Jennifer,
Love comes
all shapes
Sizes!

2020

ONE-Eighty

By
Teri Kay

Love always
Comes full Circle!.

Teri Kay

Teri Kay

Dedication

To my amazing and loving husband and partner of the
last nineteen years-
Kevin, you are my rock.
My stability in a world of constant one-eighties. I
wouldn't want to be spinning in this whirlwind with
anyone else but you.

Teri Kay

Marry Me
The Boy is Mine
Save a Horse Ride a Cowboy
Somebody to Love
Can't Stop the Feeling
A Thousand Years
She's Got a Way
Twist in my Story
The Way You Look Tonight
Parallel Lines
The Difference
Hotel Key
Break Up in the End

Teri Kay

Connor

"**D**ADDY!" MY FIVE-YEAR-old daughter, London, bursts through the door with her infectious laughter I look forward to every Friday evening.

"Munchkin!" I pick her up pulling her into one of my famous bear hugs. It kills me to think my baby girl is soon going to be too big for me to pick up like this.

"Hey, Dad," my oldest daughter says moping in behind my ex-wife.

"Well, don't you look cheerful?" I joke with her.

"You won't either after Mom talks to you."

"Harper! Enough," my ex, Eva, says.

7

"What's she talking about?" I ask.

"Girls go put your things away while I talk to your dad for a few minutes."

"What the hell is going on, Eva? Why is Harper so upset?"

"I'm being transferred, Connor."

"Ok. We've always known transfer was a possibility, which is why I freelance. I've always told you not to worry about it. I will always be there for you and the kids."

EVA AND I WERE *high school sweethearts. I played baseball and wrote for the school newspaper; she was a cheerleader and a total computer nerd. We fell hard and fast our junior year and became inseparable. After graduation, we both planned to attend Washington State, get a small apartment and enjoy the next chapter in our lives together.*

Plans all changed when we realized we had become the cliché high school couple who gets pregnant on prom night. Instead of living on our own, we moved into her parents' pool house. Eva's pregnancy was difficult, and the doctor soon ordered her on best rest, resulting in her having to quit school.

Seven months later, Harper Leigh Evans was born. My eight-pound bundle of joy was amazing and perfect. I knew from that moment forward, I needed to do everything in my power to make life spectacular for my girls. I doubled up on my classes during the day, so I could graduate early and delivered pizzas at night. We barely saw each other, but Eva knew I was trying to start a life for us.

Staying home with Harper was difficult for my girlfriend. Eva had been taking some online courses for computer programming and was quite good at it. The day I came home from school and she was sitting at the counter with paperwork in hand, I knew things were about to change.

"I want to join the army," she said.

"Excuse me?"

"Just hear me out. I'm good with computers and figuring shit out with the internet. The army could offer me some great opportunities. Us. Us some great opportunities. Housing, benefits, employment. They even help with college."

"Don't we have to be married for me to live on base with you?" I asked.

"Is that a problem?"

"Not at all, baby. I was waiting to make it a perfect day for you."

"All I need is you and our family."

Six weeks later, my entire world did a one-hundred-eighty-degree turn. There I stood on the sidewalk, holding my ten-month-old baby girl, waving my new wife off to boot camp. Luckily, both our parents had been supportive with our decisions. Whenever I needed any help with Harper, it was always the grandmas to the rescue.

For the next three years, we struggled, but they were some of the best times of our lives. Eva's computer skills were quickly noticed by her superiors. She took classes, was trained, and began moving up the ranks. A few years later she was promoted to captain and I landed a job at Seattle Explorer Magazine writing their sports column. To celebrate, we planned our long overdue honeymoon to London.

Nine months later, my second daughter was born. I thought the birth of our second child may slow Eva down, but it seemed to be just the opposite. With cyberterrorism on the rise, my wife and her position seemed to be more in demand than ever. While Eva was traveling the world training in cyber operations, I quit my job, stayed at home with the girls, and did some freelance work on the side.

Teri Kay

About a week after London's fourth birthday, my life did another wonderful one-hundred-eighty-degree turn. Pulling up to the house after picking the girls up from school, I saw Eva's car in the driveway. I didn't think much of it, since she often came home early the Friday's she was in her office and not out in the field.

When I walked in and saw her sitting at the kitchen table with papers in hand and tears streaming down her face, I knew things were not ok.

"Girls, go put Bubba in the backyard. We're going to grandma's in a bit for dinner."

I sat down at the table across from my wife and she couldn't even bring her eyes up to meet mine.

"What's going on, baby?"

"Connor, you are my best friend and I love you very much, but—" she paused as she fought back the onset of tears. Eva slid the papers across the table to me.

"These are divorce papers. What the hell, Eva? I had no idea we were even having problems." I was blindsided. I felt sick to my stomach.

"This is truly one of those 'it's not you, it's me' reasons," she tried to explain.

"This is bullshit! I've done nothing but support you and raise our kids while you're off traveling the world, falling in love with god knows whom."

"I'm sorry, Connor. I really am," Eva cried.

"Wait? So, there is someone else? You have got to be kidding me." I was shouting by this point.

"No, it's not what you think."

"Then explain it to me, Eva."

"I've never cheated on you, Connor. I've never gone behind your back. I do have feelings for someone else, though, which made me realize how far apart we've grown."

"So, who's the lucky soldier? Anyone I know? Someone you work with?"

"It's someone in my office."

"An office affair is why you choose to spend long hours away from your family?"

"Connor, I'm in love with my secretary."

It takes me a second to register what Eva has just said. "Your secretary is a woman," I state, sounding like an idiot.

"Yeah, Heather is a woman."

"Which makes you — "

"Yes, Connor. I'm a lesbian. Or maybe I'm bi-sexual. I don't know. This is all new to me."

"When did you figure this out?" I asked.

"About a year ago."

"A year ago!"

"Are you mad?" she asked.

"Yeah, I'm pissed. You've been lying to me for a year. What did you expect me to say — Oh, Eva, I'm so happy for you and your new lifestyle?"

"Connor — "

I stop her before she can say anything else. "We've been together almost half our lives and yet you couldn't be truthful with me.

"I'm sorry, Connor."

"You sure are."

11

"I'M BEING TRANSFERRED TO Thailand. Heather, the kids, and I leave in two weeks," Eva explains.

"Excuse me? Like hell you are."

"Connor, please don't make this difficult."

"Difficult? We have shared custody, Eva. Fifty-fifty. You can't just take the girls and move across the world. I never fought you on anything during the divorce, but I will for sure fight you on this. There is no way in hell I'm going to let Heather raise my daughters in Thailand, while you're off working eighty hours a week on some secret mission."

"You want me to just leave my daughters behind? With you? You know nothing about raising girls," she snaps at me.

"I've been with both the girls since the day they were born so you could run off and pursue your military career. I was with them every day of their lives until you decided to become a lesbian and divorce me. Don't even start with me saying I don't know how to raise my children."

"Do I get a say in this?" Harper interrupts us from the hallway.

"Harper, this decision doesn't involve you. Go back with your sister," Eva says.

"It does involve her. Come down here, sweet pea," I say.

"Mom, I don't want to go to Thailand. I just started middle school and I don't want to leave my friends, or Dad, or Nana and Papa."

"But you're ok leaving me?" Eva asks.

"No Mom, but you're leaving us. We're not leaving you. Seattle is my home and I don't want to go." I can see the heartbreak in my daughter's eyes as she's telling her mother she doesn't want to move with her.

Wiping the tears from Harper's eyes, her mother tells her she just wants her to be happy. "Go get London. Let's ask your sister what she would like to do."

Daniella

"DO WE REALLY HAVE to move, Mommy?" Aaron asks me for the hundredth time this morning.

"I'm sorry baby. You know we do. Trust me, you'll love Washington," I reassure him.

"Is it warm like here?"

"No, it's definitely colder than Hawaii."

"Then I don't want to go. I hate the cold," my five-year-old little man tries to protest.

"I'll keep you warm with my special hot cocoa and warm snuggle hugs." I pull my son on my lap and hug him tight.

"Mommy?"

"Yeah, baby?"

"Are you scared?"

"A little."

"I'll be brave for both of us. Daddy always says, when he isn't here, I'm the little man of the house and men are brave."

"Thank you, baby. That makes me feel better. I love you."

"I love you too, Mommy."

One week later, I'm tightly holding Aaron's small hand as we board our flight from Honolulu to Seattle. When I left Washington eight years ago, I had no intention of ever returning. After my ex-boyfriend and I broke up, there was nothing for me there, except for the few friends I had made. On a whim, I up and moved to Honolulu to sell huts on the beach.

The island became my saving grace when I wasn't sure I wanted to see the sun anymore. Makoa had become my sunshine. After the tumultuous relationship with Jimmy, I needed someone with a kind soul. Makoa Aaron Kahele became that man for me. My soulmate.

"Mommy?" My thoughts are interrupted by his tiny little voice. "Can I sit by the window? I want to see the ocean for the last time."

"Dude, stop being so dramatic. The beach is only thirty minutes from our new house in Washington."

"What does dramatic mean?"

"Silly. Stop being silly. Now sit, buckle up and get comfortable. We have six hours until we land in Seattle," I explain.

Not long after liftoff, Aaron snuggles up against me and falls asleep. As I run my fingers through his bouncy little curls, I realize how much he is starting to look like his father. Dark, sandy-blonde hair, dark Hawaiian-tanned skin, and the exact same deep brown eyes. He will be the spitting image of my husband.

Thinking of Mak, I too, drift off to sleep.

"Momma, what else do we need for Makoa's party next week?" I ask my mother-in-law, who is hosting the welcome home party for my husband's return from overseas. Her house is much better suited than ours

on base. A huge piece of land, right on the ocean, covered in lush Hawaiian plants and flowers. Honestly, it's my dream home.

"I think we're finally good. Tables and chairs will be delivered Wednesday. Papa and I have all the food handled. You and little man have the decorations taken care of?" she asks, scooping her grandson up in her arms.

"We certainly do. Don't we, buddy?"

"Yup!" my rambunctious four-year-old shouts as loud as he can.

"I'll be so glad when Mak is home and can help get some of the energy out of this guy," I say, tickling Aaron's stomach causing him to wiggle out of his grandmother's arms.

"Auntie, we're taking the kids to the beach. Nalani wants her cousin to come play. Can we bring Aaron?"

Helen, my mother-in-law, looks at me for approval. I nod. I trust the neighbors around here with my child at times more than I trust myself. Before I can even say goodbye, Aaron and Nalani are running hand in hand to the beach.

"I'll bring him home later. Why don't you go pick out something special for yourself for Mak's homecoming?" She winks at me. We both laugh.

Helen and I have developed a strong bond over the last six years. She, too, is an island transplant, actually growing up in Texas. Her father was in the Marine Corps and was transferred to the base in Honolulu when she was fifteen. It was there she met Lani Kahele, a local surfer boy, who stole her heart. For them, just like Makoa and me, it was love at first sight.

"Go. Find something naughty to tease my son. I'm ready for another grandchild," she teases.

"Eww." I laugh. "I'll see you later tonight."

My husband of five years is a proud captain in the United States Marine Corps. He has been in the Middle East for the last four months, and *we are so excited he's finally getting to come home for a while. I know his service and flight expertise are necessary, but damn I miss him more than I thought humanly possible.*

I pull into the small shopping plaza located a few blocks from the Honolulu Mall. I recently found an adult store, inconspicuously tucked away in a corner, when I needed to replace my 'battery operated boyfriend'. I was surprised to see the wide assortment they had of lingerie for curvy women. So, I figured this may be my best shot for finding something sexy to fit these hips.

Browsing through the selection, I can't help but giggle at some of the pieces. I hold up a gorgeous white corset, but from the looks of all the snaps and buttons, I'd need a team of people to get myself into this. Next, I grab a piece with so many loops and ties, I think Mak may get tangled trying to get me out of it.

Then I see it, displayed gorgeously on the mannequin and even in my husband's favorite color. A simple red baby doll nightie, completely open on the sides, laced together with one simple tie. It's what I like to think of as grown sexy.

"Makoa will go crazy when he sees me in this," I say to myself. Though I could be wearing a potato sack and my husband would still go crazy. I grab the lingerie and a few extra goodies to make his homecoming a little more special.

Driving home, I stop and grab a late lunch off one of the beachside food trucks in Waikiki. I can't believe it was six years ago when Makoa and I met on this same beach. A young surfer boy barely old enough to drink. Even though I was three years older than him and jaded at the time from a bad break-up, it never phased him. He loved me for me.

What I wasn't aware of when we met was Mak wanted to follow in his grandfather's footsteps and be a Marine. He was scheduled to leave for boot camp two weeks later. We spent two weeks wrapped in each other's arms learning everything we could about each other.

We met when I was at my lowest and he knew it. Each morning, when he picked me up for our day together, I was greeted with various exotic Hawaiian flowers. For whatever reason, Makoa was upset I didn't have a favorite flower. He said every beautiful woman should have a favorite flower and was on a mission to find mine. Each day, he would bring me a flower more beautiful than the last. I didn't want to choose a favorite, afraid he'd stop coming.   Knowing our time together was limited, we made the most out of every minute. We spent the days laughing, while he tried to teach me how to surf and I hopelessly kept falling into the ocean. Each evening, we'd retreat to the privacy of my room and make love until our bodies collapsed upon one another.

The morning before he left for San Diego, Makoa greeted me with a single hibiscus.

"This is my favorite flower, he explains, because of what it means. If a woman wears this flower behind her right ear, it means she's single and open to promises. Now, if she wears it behind her left ear, it means she is taken and uninterested in attracting a man."

Mak handed me the flower and without hesitation, I slipped it behind my left ear. That was the first time he told me he loved me. Three months later, Mak sent me a ticket to come to his boot camp graduation in San Diego with his parents and sister, Leilani. I had no idea that night at dinner, he planned on proposing. Even though our relationship happened so damn quick, everything about it is fucking perfect.

Within six months, we were married and pregnant with our first child, Aaron Kalani Kahele. Even though it's difficult dealing with little man on my own some days, we are so proud of the service Makoa is giving our country.

Teri Kay

Knowing I still have a few hours until my mother-in-law is scheduled to bring Aaron back home, I want to take advantage of the afternoon and do nothing. I grab my kindle, pour a large glass of wine, and slide myself into the plumeria-scented bubble bath I've drawn.

When the water finally gets cold, I dry off and decide to make sure my new lingerie fits these childbearing curves. I slip the cool material over my head, letting the nightie cascade over my body. Holy shit. This is sexy. I'm even getting turned on just seeing myself in it.

Quarter after five and I hear the doorbell ring. Huh? Helen must be bringing Aaron home a little earlier than we talked about. Usually she calls. I throw a robe over my new lingerie and head to the door. Mak has taught me to always look through the peephole. Even though we live on base you can never be too careful.

Two men in uniform are standing at my door waiting for me to answer.

I crack the door open just enough to peek my head through. "Yes?"

"Mrs. Kahele?"

"Yes. I'm Mrs. Kahele. What's this about?" *I ask.*

"Can we come in please?" *the older officer asks.*

"Of course. Coffee? Tea?" *I nervously offer. There are only two reasons superior officers come to your home and neither one of them are good.*

"No thank you. Can we sit please?"

"Ma'am, I'm sorry to inform you of this, but your husband, Captain Makoa Aaron Kahele, was killed last night in a helicopter crash."

"No, you must be mistaken. My husband is scheduled home next week. He will be coming home to his family."

"I'm so sorry ma'am. His unit was doing a routine patrol of the area and the helicopter he was aboard crashed. All the soldiers on board were killed."

"No, no, no!"

"Miss. Miss." The older lady next to me is shaking me awake. "You were screaming in your sleep. I think you were having a nightmare."

"Oh, my goodness. I'm so sorry. I hope I didn't disturb you," I say.

"You're fine sweetie."

I re-adjust Aaron, so I can attempt to regain feeling in my arm, which has gone completely numb from the dead weight of a five-year-old. Looking at my watch, I realize we only have ninety minutes left until we land. I'm so thankful Aaron has slept almost the entire flight. The last eight months have been just as hard for him as they have been for me. And now, I'm pulling his life into another one-eighty.

"Hi Mommy," his sweet little voice says while attempting to yawn at the same time.

"Hey baby. Sleep good?"

"Yeah. How much longer?"

"About an hour."

"K. I'm gonna watch a movie."

"Go for it, buddy. Need my help?"

"Nope."

LANDING IN SEATTLE, IT'S raining. A chilly rain. So different from the tropics of Hawaii. I know these changes are going to be so hard for Aaron, but I hope he understands I'm only trying to do what's best for us.

With the help of Addyson, one of the few friends I remained in contact with after I left Seattle, I've been given a chance to start again. She and her fiancé, Josh, offered up their guest room until I can find a home, helped me get Aaron enrolled in an excellent school, and most importantly, gave me a job.

"Daniella!" An overly excited high-pitched voice yells through the baggage area. I wave letting her know I've heard along with everyone else in the airport. We meet in the middle, and she gives me a reassuring hug, letting me know everything's going to be just fine.

"And you must be Aaron," she says kneeling down to his level. He just nods. I've never seen my son act shy before. "Well, your mom told me you are a big football fan."

"I am. I wanna play just like my daddy did," he proclaims.

"Do you have a favorite team?" she asks.

"No, because Hawaii didn't have a team."

"Well, here in Seattle we have a pretty awesome team. I sold a house to a player this month and I told him I was having a new little fan moving in with me soon. And he gave me this."

Addy holds out a brand-new Seattle Seahawks jacket for Aaron and his little face just lights up.

"This is from a real football player?" Aaron asks.

"Sure is."

"So, cool. Thanks Auntie." Aaron throws his arms around Addy's neck and gives her a hug. "I like you. You smell pretty. Can we go get my toys now?"

"I think he's going to be just fine," Addy whispers to me.

"It's not him I'm worried about."

"You're gonna be just fine too."

Teri Kay

Conner

CHAPTER ONE

"Marry Me"

4 months later

"I'M SO GLAD YOU'RE here." I haven't seen my best friend Nicolette in over two months. She moved to Spokane about a year ago to help take care of her grandmother.

"I wouldn't miss Harper's twelfth birthday for anything," she says.

"This is her first boy/girl party and she is completely freaking out over it," I explain.

"Has Eva been much help?"

"My ex-wife wasn't helpful with these kinds of things when she lived in the country. She's even less helpful over seven thousand miles away."

"I still can't see what you ever saw in her."

"Don't start, Nic."

"What? She never liked me either and you know it."

"It's because you were always the cute girl next door who she was totally jealous of," I say squeezing her cheeks.

"I am kinda cute, huh?" Nicolette giggles.

"C'mon, shorty. Let's go get your bags."

Nicolette lived across the street from me my entire life. Our moms were best friends and we were both only children, so the two of us grew up doing everything together. When I started dating Eva, the two of them would practically claw each other's eyes out every time they were in a room together. Throughout the years, their relationship never improved, yet it never stopped Nicolette from being my best friend. Since my divorce, she's become my rock.

"Auntie Nic! Auntie Nic!" My daughters start screaming from the front porch as soon as my car pulls in the driveway.

"Baby girls! Get your butts over here and give me my hugs I've been missing." The three embrace in a crazy group hug as I grab Nicolette's baggage out of the trunk.

"You get to sleep in my room and I'm gonna cuddle with Daddy," London clearly states.

"Lucky duck. Your daddy is a fantastic cuddler," she says.

"I know! He's like one of those giant teddy bears you win at the fair."

"Really? You think I'm like a teddy bear?" I ask.

"Well, you are kind of squishy," she says poking me in my stomach. You gotta love the honesty of a five-year-old.

"Alright, Miss London. How about you show me to my room in this new big house of yours."

"I'll give you the full tour. Starting with my room since it's the best." London giggles her contagious laugh.

Last month, I was finally able to purchase my first home. With the girls living with me full time now, the two-bedroom apartment wasn't cutting it anymore. We needed something bigger.

I found the perfect fixer-upper for my growing family on a small piece of land in the Seattle suburb of Redmond. Walking up to the house, it was obvious it needed work, and I am not the handiest of people. Yet when I saw the floor to ceiling windows in every room, each with its own spectacular view of the surrounding woods, I knew this was the house I wanted to raise my girls in.

"Your house is gorgeous," Nicolette says, plopping down on my bed next to me now that London finally gave her a moment's peace.

"You saw it on video chat when I bought it, goofball."

"I know. But everything looks better in person. And you're supposed to say thank you."

"Thank you," I say with obvious deflation.

"Spill it," she demands.

"It's nothing."

"Oh, don't be the girl in this relationship now. Tell me what's going on."

I get up and shut the door because I don't need my daughters hearing me. "Nic, this is so much harder than I thought."

"What is? Planning a birthday party?"

"Really?"

"Sorry. I'm just teasing. No one said being a single dad was going to be easy, but it's sure as fuck better than letting your kids move to Thailand."

"I know. I wouldn't be able to bear not being able to see them for weeks or months at a time. Sometimes I just suck at all this."

"You're doing fine, Connor. Those two precious girls adore you. And they chose you. They both chose to stay here with you, remember that. All they see is the wonderful father who would do anything to make them happy."

"Thanks. I kinda needed a Nicolette pep talk."

"I know. Remember, I know you better than anyone Mr. Playboy," Nicolette teases.

"Don't call me that," I respond, rolling my eyes at her.

"Oh c'mon. You know the story is hysterical."

"Your mother walked in on me reading your dad's playboy. Not hysterical if you're the eleven-year-old kid from next door."

"Whatever. We still laugh about it."

"Who the hell is we?"

"Me and my mom. Sometimes your mom too."

"Oh my god. Is this a regular story you all tell?"

"Yeah, kinda."

I shake my head at her. What a best friend she is. "Have you started dating?"

"There's a subject I don't even want to talk about," I flatly proclaim.

"That bad?"

"I seriously don't know how you've done it for so many years."

"It's fun if you meet the right people," she says.

"Obviously, I'm not meeting the right people."

"Dad!" We're interrupted with screams from another room.

"Let's go see what the screaming is all about, but we're not done talking about this."

"Yeah, Nic, we are."

From the upstairs landing, I can see the excitement starting to ensue below me. My daughters are circling boxes just delivered by the postman.

"Daddy, can we open them please?" London begs.

"Are they for you? It is Harper's birthday. And who are they from?"

"They're from Mom. She sent packages to both of us."

"Alright. Go ahead," I tell them.

Like two frenzied animals they start tearing apart the boxes. It's been close to three months since their mother moved to Thailand, and I know the girls miss her terribly. But like any other woman, presents always help.

I notice a disappointed look on London's face. "What's up, munchkinbutt?"

"It's just a computer plug thing taped to another box," her little deflated face says.

"It's a flash drive. We're supposed to watch it, stupid," Harper says.

"Don't start with the name calling. Go turn on my computer, we'll see what's on the flash drive and open the rest of the boxes."

Loading up the drive, I see one file which is titled "Watch Me". With a click of the mouse, a video of my ex-wife and her new girlfriend pops up. Eva is just as gorgeous now as she was when I met her sixteen years ago. Long, jet-black hair, stormy gray eyes, and amazing olive-colored skin. Her father was Italian and her mother Greek. Eva received her beauty from both.

Harper hits play. "Hi my gorgeous daughters. Hi Connor. I miss you all so much. Harper, I'm sorry I couldn't be there for your birthday, but by now you know how the Army works. I'll get some time off this summer and get to come back to Seattle for a few weeks. I cannot wait to see you both. Now pause here and go open the gifts and then come back and I'll explain them."

I pause the video as Nicolette arranges the boxes on the floor and helps the girls open them. The excitement on her face makes me laugh. You would think there were gifts for her in there. Each box contained an intricately crafted teddy bear, a beaded purse and elephant jewelry.

After each package was opened, I restarted Eva's video. "The bears are Nantakwang Cushion Animals. Each pattern is unique, and no two animals are the same. When Heather and I went to Bangkok a few weeks ago, we met these women from a native tribe living in Northern Thailand. The purses and jewelry are all handcrafted by the women and their families. I hope you like your gifts. We did our best to choose gifts as special and unique as you two are. Girls, they are sending me on assignment and I won't be able to talk to you for a while. I love you both so much. Take care of your dad. Talk to you soon girls." She blows them kisses and ends the video.

"Harper, you ok?" I ask.

"Yeah, I just really miss her," she says.

"I have an idea!" Nicolette shouts out of nowhere.

"Alright, let's hear it." I laugh.

"Sushi and dress shopping."

"Yes!" Both the girls agree.

"Oh, how did I get so lucky?" I sarcastically joke.

"I don't know Daddy, but you are pretty lucky to have us," London says grabbing my hand and pulling me toward the door.

At dinner, Harper incessantly talks Nicolette's ears off; everything from the break-up of One Direction, to which boys are coming to the party, to unicorns. I can see how much she needs an older female, who's not her grandmother, to talk to. It's moments like these I hate Eva for choosing her career over her family.

"So, Dad, I was thinking. Can we split up for a while? Nic said she'd let me pick out a new outfit for my birthday party tomorrow. I thought you could take London and help her pick out something to wear."

"What, you don't want to go shopping with your dear old dad?"

"No, I... uh..."

"Honey, I'm teasing you. Go. Nic, make it appropriate. She's twelve, not twenty-one."

Walking out of the restaurant, I come up behind Nicolette and whisper thank you into her ear.

"I know she needs some girl time. Why don't you take London home when you're done? We'll just catch an Uber. We may be a while." My best friend grabs my oldest by her hand and pulls her off into the mall. When Nicolette looks back to shoo me off, her smile catches me a bit off guard.

Nicolette and I have been together since we were born; we have pictures of us in the bath together as babies. As a teenager, I always thought she was cute. As an adult, I know she's pretty, but her smile is downright fucking sexy.

"Daddy, are you even listening to me?" London says, tugging at my shirt.

"I'm sorry, munchkin, I wasn't. Tell me again."

"I want a Minion dress."

"Ok, any reason why?" I ask. I love hearing London's answers. Ever since she started kindergarten, her vocabulary has blossomed, and the things this girl says crack me up.

"Well, there's this boy in my class, Brian, and he doesn't speak any English. But he learned the word banana and he says it like all the time. And Ms. Johnston said he sounds like a Minion and he makes me laugh so I want a Minion dress."

"Ok then. Let's go get you a Minion dress." I laugh scooping my daughter up in my arms and taking her to go find whatever her little heart desires. My mom says I spoil my daughters, but after Eva's leaving, I feel they need to be spoiled.

By nine the next morning, my house is already in complete chaos. My parents and Eva's family all arrived early to help with the decorating and cooking for the thirty pre-teens about to raid my backyard.

I knew this party was going to take some work and planning, but when Harper told me she wanted a Harry Potter themed birthday party, I almost jumped for joy. She is definitely my little girl.

We set up the backyard like a castle, having it divided into the four houses. As the kids arrive, they randomly get sorted and are given their colored robes to wear. We also realized this was a way of ensuring no kid felt left out when being chosen for a game later. I know that feeling all too well.

We set up different rooms in our house to match scenes from the books: Diagon Alley, Gringotts bank, Hagrid's house. Each room with an activity or riddle each house had to solve where they would earn coins to go "shopping" with later. I must admit, I really outdid myself on this one.

Hours later, tucking Harper into bed, she throws her arms around my neck like she did when she was little. "Thank you, Dad. Today was perfect. I love you."

"I love you too, sweet pea. You know I'd do anything to see your beautiful smile." I kiss her on the forehead before exiting her room.

Walking into the backyard, I see Nicolette relaxing on my double lounge chair drinking a beer.

"Now that looks good," I say.

"It is. Here." She hands me a bottle from the cooler on the other side of her.

"Thank you."

"For what?"

"Being here. Helping me with the girls."

"Connor, you know I love these girls like they are my own. I wouldn't be anywhere else. I tucked London into her bed. Is it alright if I crash with you?"

I hesitate, which causes her to scrunch her brow. "What? You don't want to share a bed with me?" she asks.

"No. Why would you say that?"

"You hesitated."

"Whatever. No, I didn't. Grab those beers. Let's go watch a movie," I say changing the subject.

We both slip into sweats and T-shirts and crawl into my plush king-size bed. The last time I shared a bed with Nicolette was when we were nine. We were on a family camping trip and neither one of us wanted to share a tent with our parents. It wasn't long after, our parents discovered we both started liking the opposite sex and it probably wasn't appropriate anymore.

"Binge or movie?" I ask.

31

"Hmmmm…movie. Something scary," she suggests.

"I think I know just the movie." I scroll through the Netflix queue and find Nic's favorite movie from middle school.

"Holy shit! Really? *Disturbing Behavior*? I can't believe you remember."

"I probably remember much more than you think," I say.

Nicolette curls up in bed next to me and uses my chest as a pillow. I love how after almost twenty years this movie still makes her jump in the same places. Each time she jumps, Nic curls her body up a little closer to mine.

I've always wondered what Nicolette and I would be today if it had been her I started dating all those years back instead of Eva. In all the years we've been friends, we have never been single at the same time. I was a late bloomer, and by then, many of the boys at school had already claimed Nicolette as their own. Then I met Eva during our junior year and was with her from that point on.

Several times throughout the evening, I consider kissing her. Something causes me to chicken out each time. If she rejects me, will I lose my best friend? But if she reciprocates, could this be the best thing ever? Before I get a chance to find out, she is gently snoring on my chest.

The next morning, I awake to an empty bed, which I'll admit is slightly disappointing. It's been a while since I've woken up to a gorgeous girl in bed next to me. I wonder if all my thoughts about Nicolette were just because I'm horny and haven't had sex in nearly five months, or because for the first time I see her as more than just the cute girl next door.

From the landing, I can hear the sweet muffled giggles coming from the kitchen. Nicolette and the girls are already up and making breakfast and it smells delicious.

"Good morning, my beautiful ladies," I bellow, walking into the kitchen. I kiss London, Harper and Nic all on the cheek before pouring my first cup of morning coffee.

"Morning Daddy," the girls say in unison.

"Morning handsome," Nicolette says handing me a plate of French toast.

I sit at the table and start to eat my breakfast. "Wow, girls! This is amazing. Did Auntie Nic share this recipe with you?"

"Yup. She said her chef boyfriend taught it to her," London exclaims.

"Boyfriend, huh?" I ask.

"Uh, yeah," she stammers. "I met him a couple months ago at a restaurant I was hired to consult at."

"Cool. What time do you have to be at the airport?" I ask flatly.

"Noon. You ok?"

"Yup. We'll leave about ten, so I can drop the girls off at my parents."

"No, Dad you said I could start babysitting when I turned twelve. I'm ready. Let me watch London when you go to the airport," Harper says.

"I'm not sure about that yet."

"C'mon Dad. It's only like an hour and a half. We'll be fine."

"I know you will. You both are good girls. I just hate you're growing up so fast."

There was an awkward silence hanging in the air the entire drive to the airport.

"What's up, Connor?"

"Why didn't you tell me you had a boyfriend? We don't keep things from each other."

"Are you really that upset about it?"

"A little, yeah."

"I didn't want to tell you about Brad just yet."

"Brad? His name is Brad," I interrupt.

"Stop, Connor. He's a nice guy. I know dating has been difficult for you and I just didn't want to seem like I was rubbing it in your face or anything."

"So, you'd rather lie. How nice of you."

"C'mon, you're overreacting. What has got you all bothered?" Nicolette asks.

"Why was it never us?" I ask.

"What?" She was obviously taken off guard by my question.

"I'm sorry. Never mind."

"Connor, I love you, but you're my best friend. The last thing I'd ever want is to do anything to risk our friendship. I need you. A break up would be devastating to us."

"Maybe we wouldn't break up. Maybe we are meant to be together."

"I need you too much to ever try. Connor, you're like…like a brother to me. Soon you will find someone who is just as special to you as Brad is to me."

All I can think is thank god I didn't try and kiss her last night.

CHAPTER TWO
Daniella

"Y OU KNOW YOU DON'T have to move," Addyson tells me as I'm signing the closing papers on my new home. "Josh and I love having you back in Seattle."

"I know. Thank you. But you're not the one sharing a bed with a five-year-old who kicks." I laugh.

"True. But he's so cute."

"He reminds me more and more of Makoa every day." I fight back the tears stinging my eyes. I'm glad I'm in the privacy of my own office alone with my best friend.

"He'd be proud of you, Dani," Addyson reassures me. With those words, the floodgates open. The tears begin to stream uncontrollably down my face. "Oh honey, I didn't mean to make you cry."

"I...I know. You didn't. I've just been holding it all in for so long. I just miss him so damn much. I feel like the universe keeps telling me something. It sucks."

"And what is that?" she asks with an almost snide tone.

"That I'm not supposed to be in love."

"Bullshit, Daniella and you know it!" she yells at me. You have to love the friends who don't hold anything back.

"Really? I never had any real relationships in high school because I was moved around so much and the few guys I did date turned out to be pieces of shit. And we won't talk about Jimmy."

"Jimmy was a twat waffle." Her comment causes me to shoot soda straight out my nose.

"Holy shit. I love that word." I laugh.

"You've never heard it before?"

"No, but I will be using it again."

"Well, he was, and you know it. I heard he got Catalina Montana pregnant and left her. You are so lucky you got rid of that toxic piece of shit."

I met Addyson, Josh, and Jimmy while we were taking our real estate classes together. The four of us thought we could take Seattle's booming housing market by storm. Over time, we noticed Jimmy seemed to close double the amount of deals the rest of us were. No one knew how or why, but the lender from our firm was approving each one of Jimmy's deals with ease.

One afternoon, about two months after I moved in with Jimmy, I came home from work early due to some bad sushi. I was surprised to see my boyfriend's car in the driveway but figured dinner from last night must have hit him too. Until I saw a purse on the table, high heels by the couch, and a black, lace bra thrown onto the floor. The moans coming from the bedroom were undeniably loud. And not mine.

I throw the door of our bedroom open to see the perky little B-cup tits of Catalina Montana, the agency's lender, bouncing up and down as she rides my boyfriend reverse cowgirl style. I didn't scream or yell or throw any kind of fit. I just simply looked at the two of them, laughed and walked out. Apparently, Jimmy needed to use his dick to sell houses.

"I wonder what ever happened to him," I say.

"Do you? Do you really care?" Addy asks.

"No, not really. But I'd like to thank the twat waffle."

"Thank him? For what?"

"Taking me out for bad sushi."

"Alright, sister fill me in because I'm confused as fuck."

"If Jimmy wouldn't have taken me to the cheap sushi place, I wouldn't have gotten sick and gone home early from work to find him and Catalina fucking. Which wouldn't have sent me over the edge and to Hawaii where I met Mak, learned what real love was, and had my precious baby boy."

"Well, damn! I'll drink to that. Let's get this paperwork submitted and go out and celebrate you buying your first house."

"I can't. I have to pick Aaron up from the afterschool program by five."

"Hey Josh!" Addy leans back and screams into the hallway.

"Yeah, baby?"

"Dani and I want to go celebrate the closing of her house. Will you pick up Aaron for her? Maybe you guys could go see the Lego movie or something."

"Oh, Josh, you don't have to do that. We can celebrate another night," I say.

"I think I can handle kid duty for a night. Plus, it's good practice if we ever decide to finally have kids."

"We'll only be a couple hours." I already feel guilty for leaving Aaron for any amount of time.

"It will be fine. You deserve a night out," Josh says putting his hands on my shoulders, reassuring me my boy is in good hands. "Go home, get all prettied up like you girls do, I'll call an Uber to come get you, and enjoy your night."

"Thank you, Josh. You are one of the greats." I stand on my tiptoes and kiss his cheek.

He does the cocky shoulder wipe. "Yeah, they don't make 'em like me anymore."

An hour later, Addyson and I have our nineties iTunes mix blaring, wine glasses full, and are raiding our closets trying to find something sexy to wear.

"I don't think I can go out," I pout.

"Just like Aaron, so dramatic. Why not?" Addy laughs at me, moping into her room.

"I don't have a damn thing to wear. Nothing I own is sexy. Sexy stopped for me in 2012."

"What, you stopped being sexy when you became a mom?" she asks.

"Yeah, kind of. Mak was overseas most of the time and when he was home we were usually doing things with Aaron. And even though my husband found my baby curves sexy, I still have a challenging time seeing myself as such."

"Alright, come with me." Addy grabs my hand and drags me back to my room. "Lesson number one. It's not what you wear it's how you wear it. What is your favorite thing in your entire closet?"

I pulled out a pair of boyfriend jeans which fit my butt perfectly. "But these are comfortable, not sexy."

"Just wait. Pick out three shirts. A comfortable one, one everyone else likes, and the one you think makes your boobs look best."

"What?" I question.

"Do it," she demands. By this time the wine is starting to kick in and we are both laughing at her playing real life Barbie with me.

I pick out three shirts, like my little dictator commands. "Now, what shoes make you feel sexy?"

Before I can pick out my shoes, Addy and I are interrupted with a Facetime call from Josh.

"Hey Josh. Is everything ok?" I ask before Addy can even get a hello in.

"We're fine. Aaron just wanted to talk to you before we go out," he says.

"Hi Mom!" my son shouts popping into the frame. "Is it ok if I go out with Uncle Josh tonight?"

"Of course."

"Ok you won't be sad?" he asks. "Cause you're not with us?"

"Well, I'll miss you, but I won't be sad. Auntie Addy and I are going out too."

"Yup! Girls' night and boys' night, just like Uncle said." I'm so glad Aaron has not lost the Hawaiian custom of calling close friends and family Auntie and Uncle.

"Did Uncle say where he was taking you?"

"Mini golf and the arcade," Josh chimes in from the background. "Pizza ok for dinner?"

"Pizza's fine. Have fun on your boys' night! Thanks again Josh."

"No problem. You two try and stay out of trouble tonight."

"We're not making any promises. Love you guys," Addyson says before hanging up.

"C'mon, we have forty-five minutes before our ride gets here. Let's finish your hair and makeup and get the hell out of here," Addy says, yanking me back to her room.

Thirty minutes later, I'm standing in front of my closest mirror looking myself up and down. Addyson has done wonders for my confidence tonight. We paired my favorite jeans with an amazing cream-colored sweater from Addy's closet, since all my clothes are for island temperatures, and my cute little tan ankle boots. She put loose curls throughout my thick blonde tresses giving it a bounce I didn't even know it had. Addy knows I'm not much of a makeup person, but she applies just enough to make my eyes pop and cheeks glow.

"I don't know if I can do this," I say.

"Do what?"

"Go out. I haven't gone out since my husband died."

"Dani, tonight is two girlfriends celebrating the purchase of a new house. Not a date. I think your husband would be fine with you going out tonight."

"You're right. I'm sorry. I'm just nervous."

"Don't ever be sorry, my friend. We all grieve in our own ways."

"Thank you."

The text alert Addy receives lets us know our ride is here. "C'mon, girl. Let's go have a well-deserved girls night. You bought a house and hell I almost forgot I sold a house! Time to celebrate."

We laugh the entire ride into downtown Seattle about anything and everything. It makes me realize how much I have truly missed being surrounded by friends or just even people in general. Makoa and I were always the energy in the room. He gave me the spark to shine bright and now I must learn how to shine on my own.

"Alright ladies, we are at your destination. Your husband has also arranged for me to pick you up at one a.m. Just send me a text and let me know where you are," Frank, our driver tells us.

"Thank you. It will be somewhere right down here. We don't plan on wandering too far," Addyson says.

"Is the food at Radiator Whiskey as good as it used it to be?" I ask.

"Better. Let's start there!"

By seven on a Friday night the bar is already packed, but luckily, we're able to find two open seats tucked away in a back corner. Not the best seats in the place, but I'm just needing to get some food into my stomach before anymore alcohol does. If I remember right, the small plates here are to die for.

When the waitress brings us our signature bourbon cocktails, Addyson raises her glass. "Cheers. To old friendships and new beginnings."

"Cheers," I say, clinking my glass to hers.

"You ready for this?" she asks.

"For what? A night out?"

"Well, that too. But I meant living on your own."

"I have to be. Aaron's growing up and needs his own space. Plus, it's been a year since Mak's death. He would want me to start finding my happy again."

"I only met your husband once, but he was an amazing man. His laugh was infectious. The one thing I've always told Josh is I remember how happy he was. And now I see him in your son."

"Me too. I'm so lucky to have my little man."

"Alright! No more sad talk. Let's finish this amazing Fried Beef Lip Terrine and find a place for some dancing and maybe even some karaoke."

"Dancing, yes. Karaoke, I'm not so sure about."

"Oh, whatever. You know we sing the best *The Boy is Mine* ever." Addy laughs.

"Yeah, we were pretty good, weren't we?"

"Hell yeah, we were. C'mon let's go hit up Slick's. They still do karaoke on Friday nights."

"Sounds like we've got our plan."

There's a short line to get into the bar, but the overly muscled, tattooed bouncer waves us to the front. "Pretty women like you shouldn't have to stand out in the cold," he says in a heavy southern accent.

"Thank you," I say, as he flashes us his sexy smile.

"Ummm, damn. Can you say sex on a stick?" Addy giggles as we make our way to the bar.

"Who?"

"The bouncer. You couldn't have missed him. I know you're not looking, but you aren't blind either."

"Eh. He was alright."

"Really?"

"Yeah. I don't know. Just not my type."

"What is your type? The only two guys I've ever seen you with, Jimmy and Makoa, were opposites," Addy shouts over the horribly-loud, offkey singer on stage.

Her question makes me think. I have no idea what my type is. Jimmy was older than me, tall with sandy-blonde hair and these perfectly golden-hazel eyes. Jimmy came from money and was groomed to be Seattle white collar. Makoa was my younger Hawaiian dream. Dark hair, dark eyes, and a heart of solid gold.

"I have no idea. A guy who will buy me a drink and be satisfied with a handshake at the end of the night?" I joke.

"It's a good thing you make your own money," she teases.

"You wanna sing?" I ask attempting to change the subject.

"Of course! Together?"

"Yes. I sound like shit without you."

Addy and I head to the DJ booth to flip through the available songbook. "New or old?" she asks.

"New. I think. I don't know. I suck at picking songs."

"I'm not sure I know any of the new songs well enough yet," Addyson complains.

"Hey, while you two try and figure out what you're going to sing, mind if I put my name on the list since I know what I want to sing," a man from behind me says.

"Really? You that anxious to sing you can't wait another minute for my friend and I to pick out our song?" I ask. I look up to meet the most mesmerizing blue eyes I have ever seen. Immediately, I wanted to put my words back in my mouth. Until he spoke again.

"Look here cupcake. I'm ready to sing. And your indecisiveness is preventing me from doing that. So, pick a song or let the rest of us by," he gripes.

I look at the first song on the list and write it next to our names, *Can't Stop the Feeling* by Justin Timberlake.

"Really?" she asks.

"Mr. Rude Guy was making me so mad, I just wrote down the first thing I saw."

"You're funny. Guys in bars are jerks. Don't let them bother you. At least we know this one cause Aaron's only watched it a thousand times since you guys have been staying with us."

"And next up we have the guy who's been keeping you safe all night, Colton," the DJ announces.

Mr. Muscles bouncer guy is up next. I do have to admit his accent is kind of sexy. "Hey y'all. I'm gonna take you back to Tennessee with me tonight." He points to the DJ and *Save a Horse Ride a Cowboy* starts playing.

"Really?" Addy and I say at the same time.

"Told you. Guys that pretty usually have the ego to match," I say.

"Yeah, but I wouldn't mind taking him for a ride." She laughs.

"Ummm... hello? Again, fiancé at home."

"I didn't say I would. But I'm allowed to admire from afar."

"Next up, we have Addyson and Daniella," the DJ calls for us.

"I'm actually a little nervous," I confess.

"Whatever! This song is easy and fun. Let's go." She grabs my arm and drags me onto the stage with her.

As the music starts playing, a stupid smile is plastered across my face. I no longer see a hundred strangers staring back me. I just see Aaron and his tiny, happy face singing this song repeatedly. And for the first time in the past year, I genuinely smile. I can feel Makoa giving me strength for both our son and myself, and I know we're going to be just fine.

"O.M.G! That was so much fun," I shout coming off the stage. "Thank you, Addy. I really needed this tonight."

"I know. That's what best friends are for," she says.

"Alright, folks. It's the time you've all been waiting for," the DJ says, getting the crowd pumped up. "We haven't seen him in a while, but he's back tonight. Give a Slick's welcome back to Karaoke Connor."

Still riding on my singing high, I begin cheering for Karaoke Connor with the rest of the bar. I stop mid-clap, when I realize Connor is Mr. Rude. Figures the guy everyone in the bar loves is the same asshat who was behind me in line.

"Figures." I laugh. "C'mon, perfect time to go shoot some pool." I stand up from my chair but am stopped in my tracks when I hear the piano intro to *Somebody to Love* by Queen. Almost as if I was in a trance, I sit back down to listen to Connor sing.

"I thought we were going to shoot pool?" Addy asks.

"Shhh. Wait a minute."

During the four-and-a-half-minute song, I am unable to take my eyes off this man. Something about the way he sings his song has me locked in my seat. But as soon as it is over, I need to leave.

"Can we text the Uber? I'm ready to go," I ask Addy.

"What just happened?"

"Addyson, I need to go home. Can you please just call the Uber?"

"Sure, honey. Whatever you need," she says.

Tears stream down my face the entire ride home. Addyson tries to comfort me, but I shrug off her attempts. "Daniella, it's ok to cry. You might feel better if you talk about whatever is bothering you." I can't say anything.

Getting home, I go straight to my room and rip off the going-out clothes Addy had dressed me in and threw on my sweats and an old Marine T-shirt of Mak's. Without saying a word, I head to the kitchen and grab the bottle of tequila from the freezer. I grab a shot glass from the cabinet and pour myself two back-to-back shots.

"Pour me one," Addyson says, reappearing from the bathroom.

"Sorry," I say.

"Stop. I told you never to be sorry. Are you ready to talk about it?"

"It's gonna sound stupid."

"So? That's what best friends are for, to listen to all the stupid shit the other has to say."

"All night, I felt like Makoa was with me, giving me his happy vibes."

"What changed?"

"Mr. Rude's song," I explain.

"Alright, clue me in," she says.

"The day I met Makoa on the beach in Waikiki, I was in the middle of having a pity party for myself after finding Jimmy in bed with Catalina. *Somebody to Love* was blaring through my ear buds when Mak came running out of the water. It was like this weird cosmic sign. The sign telling me he was the man to fix my broken heart." I take another shot. "So after feeling like Mak was there with me all night and then Mr. Rude Karaoke Connor guy sang our song. It all just got too weird and I needed to get out of there."

"Wow. Yeah, I would have needed to get out of there too."

I pour us each another shot. "I mean, have you heard those damn lyrics?" I ask.

"Maybe Mak was sending you a sign," Addy says.

"Through Mr. Rude?"

"You never know." She shrugs her shoulders and laughs. "The universe is a funny bitch. C'mon, Josh and Aaron fell asleep in my bed watching Trolls. Let's finish this bottle of tequila and watch *Magic Mike*," my best friend suggests.

"Sounds like a plan to me," I say.

"So, did you happen to catch Mr. Rude's eyes?" Addy asks.

"It was kind of hard not to. Those are the kind of blue eyes only book boyfriends have."

Teri Kay

Conner
CHAPTER THREE

T HE SUN IS COMING through the crack in the curtains like it's trying to start a fire on my forehead...I feel like I swallowed a fucking cactus...and I believe someone has implanted a bass drum in my head. What the fuck happened last night?

I stumble downstairs to make myself a cup of coffee and find the Tylenol, and I find Colton snoring away on the couch. Of all the chicks at the bar last night, I end up taking home the bouncer. What the fuck is wrong with my life?

By no means am I attempting to be quiet while in the kitchen. I'm hoping to wake this guy up and get him off my couch. Colton and I met at Slick's about six months ago and became quick friends, even though we're polar opposites.

"I'm up. You can stop banging dishes around, man," he shouts from the living room.

"Sorry. Coffee?"

"Sure."

"Gotta ask. How'd you end up on my couch last night? How'd we even get to my house?"

"You don't remember shit from last night, do you?" Colton asks.

"The last thing I really remember is the feisty blonde leaving after I sang *Somebody to Love*."

"Yeah, well that hot little thing must have gotten under your skin, 'cause after she left, you started throwing back tequila shots like nobody's business."

"No wonder I feel like I swallowed a cactus. Ok, so how did we end up here?" I ask.

"You refused to get into your Uber and were actually causing quite a scene. Dude, the manager was gonna call the cops."

"Do I even want to know why?" I'm already embarrassed as hell.

"'Cause the car had a 49ers sticker across the back window." Colton laughs.

"You've got to be kidding me?"

"Nope. Then you started calling the driver an idiot for driving around Seattle with a rival team's sticker and saying she should be ashamed for calling herself a football fan."

"Her?"

"Yup, cute little twenty-three-year-old thing. Second night on the job."

"Oh, I am an asshole."

"Pretty much. I said I'd take you, so they didn't call the cops. Once we got here, you invited me in for a beer and Call of Duty," Colton explains.

"Sounds like me."

"Who's Brad?"

"I don't know a Brad besides the fact my best friend told me she's dating some guy named Brad. Why?"

"Because you kept shooting people saying 'Die, Brad, die'."

"Maybe I'm a little more worked up about Nicolette dating than I thought."

"And how long has it been since you've gotten laid?" he sarcastically asks.

"Fuck, I don't know. Six or seven months. Last night was the first night I've been out since the girls have moved in with me. Dating as a single dad is not easy."

"Maybe if you were a little nicer to the girls at the bar, one of them may have taken you home instead of me."

"Man, those two chicks in line were taking forever to pick out their song and I was ready to sing."

"Doesn't give you the right to be an asshat to two pretty ladies, either of whom could have taken you home last night."

"They both had rings. Trust me, I looked. The blonde was fucking gorgeous," I admit.

"Are you working tonight? The girls are with their grandparents until tomorrow and there's no way in hell I'm sitting around here by myself."

"No, sir, I am not. Plan on going downtown and finding some hot little thing to sink my dick into. Care to join me?"

"Why the hell not. Count me in."

"Meet me at Slick's at eight," he shouts on his way out the door.

As I'm getting dressed, it hits me I've never done the "going out and picking up chick's" thing. I was with Eva for close to fifteen years, and the few dates I've been on since then were all set ups. And tonight, I get to be the wingman for Mr. GQ himself. This should be interesting.

Running a little late, by the time I get to the bar, Colton has already found us a pool table and two insanely hot blondes. I stop by the bar, grabbing myself a beer and ordering another round for the table, before making my way over to the group.

"Connor! You finally made it," he greets me as I enter the side room.

"Damn Uber driver got lost. I ordered another round for the table."

"Awesome. Connor, meet Britney and Ashley. Girls, meet my buddy Connor."

Both girls hug me, but I could see neither is thrilled by my presence. I mean damn, I know I don't have the ironclad, muscled body Colton has, but I don't think I'm a total disappointment.

"Why don't we shoot in teams? Me and Britney against you and Ashley," Colton suggests. His attempt to divide and conquer is clearly obvious. Ashley's not bad looking, but not really the type of girl I like to date, but I could have some fun with her tonight.

It doesn't take long for me to pick up on the signs she's just not interested in me. But the biggest kick in the nuts is when she asks me if I think Colton would be up to a threesome with her and Britney.

"I'm out, man," I shout to Colton, who's dick is pressed up hard against the ass of Britney.

"What do you mean? What about Ashley?"

"Ha! Enjoy 'em both, Colt. See ya, dude." I text my Uber and make my way back home.

WRITING HAS ALWAYS BEEN my passion. Even though I earned my degree in journalism and could work at any newspaper or magazine in the state, I have been able to live my dream of being a freelance sports writer. I have been privileged enough to work on a few influential people and have earned myself a reputation, which has allowed me to keep freelance writing even after my divorce.

Today, I'm downtown starting my research for a piece I've just been hired to do by *Ganja Geek Magazine*. I've never written about pot before; being a father I usually try to keep my nose and my work fairly clean. When the editor contacted me last month and explained they were looking for someone to write an article on how the legalization of marijuana is affecting the sports community in Washington state, I was immediately interested. Not to mention they are willing to pay five grand if the article is what they are looking for. Challenge accepted.

Grabbing a coffee, I sit down at a corner booth and pull out my laptop to prepare my notes for today's interview. My meeting with Dr. Haven, a sports medicine specialist at Washington Regional Hospital, is scheduled for ten, and I am not nearly as prepared as I should be.

My attention span has been at a zero lately. It's been over two weeks since my karaoke night from hell, but I'm still feeling guilty for treating the feisty little blonde like shit. It's just not the kind of guy I am, and my behavior was so out of character. Maybe she'll show up for another karaoke night and Colton will be able to figure out who she is.

Lost in a daydream, I didn't catch my phone ringing until the last second. "Hello?"

"Mr. Evans, this is Ms. Johnston, London's teacher."

"Good morning. Is London ok?"

"Yes, she's fine. I was wondering if you'd be able to stop by my room for a quick meeting when you pick London up this afternoon. I'd like to talk to you about a few things," she explains.

"I can. See you this afternoon."

What the hell could London have gotten into this time? My daughter is only five, but she is definitely my spitfire. She reminds me so much of her mother. But as if I wasn't distracted enough as it is, now I have to worry about my daughter. I pull up my notes and get to work before Dr. Haven arrives.

Luckily, my schedule has always allowed me to put my daughters' needs first. Even after the divorce, I swore to myself I would never have my children raised by babysitters or nannies. I arrive at the school fifteen minutes before the end of the day, allowing myself enough time to find a parking spot and get checked in before making my way to the classroom.

Sitting on the playground bench, I watch Ms. Johnston in awe. I can barely handle my one kindergartner, no less twenty-three at the same time.

"Thank you for coming in this afternoon," she greets me after she dismisses the last child out the gate.

"Of course. London's progress is extremely important to me."

"C'mon, let's grab London and go sit inside." She calls my daughter in from the slide and we make our way into the overly colorful and cute classroom.

"My first concern is with London's reading," the teacher explains.

"Ok. Isn't she a fairly good reader for six?" I ask.

"She is, but she's having a difficult time understanding and remembering what she reads."

"I see. What can I do to help her?"

"Ask London questions about what she's reading or have her retell you what you read to her. She will begin to focus more on what she's reading rather than just the words she's reading."

"I can do that. You said her reading was your first concern. Is there something else going on?" I ask.

"I know London's mother moved to Thailand at the beginning of the school year. Has anything else changed recently in her life?"

"Not that I can think of. What's going on Ms. Johnston?"

"London has begun teasing, almost to the point of bullying, with a few students in our class."

"Young lady, what is going on?" I ask my daughter.

She shrugs while big tears well up in her dark-gray eyes. "No tears, London. Why are you doing these things?"

"Mr. Evans, children this young often don't know why they are acting this way. Sometimes it can be because of a change at home, an outside influence, or just simply a child is acting out to get attention."

"I, in no way, agree with London's behavior and I will get to the bottom of it. What are some of the things she's doing?"

"London tends to be bossy and likes things done her way." Like mother like daughter, I think to myself. "If she doesn't get her way she can get a bit sassy."

"Really?" I look at London who now has tears streaming down her face. "We will be having a long talk about this behavior tonight. Is there anything else I should know about?"

"London, why don't you tell your dad about making Aaron cry again today," Ms. Johnston suggests.

"Again?" I question.

"I'm not trying to be mean," she whines.

"I know. But Aaron has asked you several times to stop."

"London, what are doing?" I demand, no longer willing to play her games or accept her excuses.

"I call him Maui, Daddy. He looks just like Maui from Moana."

"Aaron started with us a couple weeks ago. He just recently moved here from Hawaii."

"I apologize Ms. Johnston. I do not tolerate bullying in any way and we will be having some lengthy discussions about this."

Walking back to the office, London is still crying. "Honey, I still love you, but I am very disappointed in your behavior. C'mon, let's head home so we can meet your sister."

Opening the office door, my eyes meet hers. What the hell? Of all the places I thought I might run into her again, the kid's school office is not one of them. The last thing I want to do is apologize for my drunken rudeness in front of the school secretary.

As we walk closer to the exit, I can't help but overhear their conversation. "Well, if she's not available then I guess I'll have to schedule a meeting. There is no reason why my five-year-old should be coming home from school crying. I'd like to know why this Landan child has been allowed to bully my son."

Oh, fuck me. Really? Of all the kids, in all the school, mine has to pick on hers.

"Ok, Ms. Kahele, I will send the message to Ms. Johnston," the secretary says.

In an awkward coincidence, we all exit the office at the same time. I can tell she's trying to high tail it out of there without talking to me. What do I say to stop her—Miss, ma'am, Ms. Kahele?

"Hey!" I shout. Great, now I continue to look like the rude asshat. She stops, turns around to look at me and gives me one of the evilest glares I've ever seen.

"What?" she quips. Damn, her feistiness is hot.

"Do you remember me from karaoke a few weeks ago?" I ask.

"How could I forget Mr. Rude?" Ouch, she is a snarky one.

"Hi, Aaron," London interrupts.

"Hi, Landan," Aaron mispronounces.

"It's London. Uh, uh, uh sound," she corrects him.

"This is Landan?" she asks her son. He nods.

"See Daddy, he's teasing me too." I can't stand seeing she somehow has developed her mother's whine.

"Saying someone's name wrong and teasing them with a cartoon character are two entirely different things, young lady. What do you need to say to your friend?"

"I'm sorry, Aaron."

"I'm sorry too. Mrs...?" I wait for her response.

"Daniella."

"I'm sorry, Daniella. First, for London's behavior. It is not how I've raised my daughter to act. And, for my behavior at Slick's. Rude behavior is not acceptable by anyone in my family."

"Thank you. We appreciate your apology, Karaoke Connor." She laughs.

"Wait, I thought it was Mr. Rude?"

ONLY SIX WEEKS AGO, Nicolette told me about her and Brad dating, two weeks later I get the call they are engaged, and now their wedding day is already here. Her theory is why wait when you know it's right. Well, that and she is constantly reminding us of her ticking biological clock.

I got to meet Brad last weekend when they came to Seattle for a weekend trip. He's a nice enough guy, but I think Nicolette is way too good for him. The guy's a pastry chef for Christ's sake. I highly doubt I'll be inviting him to join us on our next hunting trip. The guy has probably never picked up a gun in his life.

Sitting in the sports bar at the airport, I'm enjoying a beer before my flight. One of my favorite things to do in an airport is people watch and try to figure out where they're from or where they're going. People fascinate me. From the old man in the corner playing with his grandson on a tablet to the young families hauling a shit ton of kids behind them. I'm curious if people ever look at me and wonder my story? I bet most see the overweight, happy guy who's usually the life of the party. Who would guess I'm the single dad who is sad about not having someone to share his heart with?

The flight from Seattle to Spokane is just over an hour, which is just enough time to enjoy a few drinks on the plane, flirt with the stewardess, and get off before I make a fool of myself.

Nicolette had offered me the spare room at the apartment she shares with Brad, but I opted for the Hilton, with the rest of the wedding party. As much as I love my best friend and am happy for her, I'm jealous it's not me. I miss having someone to share my days with. After Eva and I divorced, I thought that someone might be Nic, but for her it's Brad.

Before settling in for the night, I video chat my daughters.

"Hi Daddy," they answer in unison.

"Hi girls. I wanted to call and tell you how much I love you before I go to sleep tonight. I probably won't get a chance to call you tomorrow."

"It's ok, Dad. You just make sure Auntie Nic has a fantastic wedding," London says.

"I'll do my best, munchkin." I laugh.

"You ok, Dad?" Harper asks.

"I'm fine, sweetie. Just tired. You guys have fun with Nana and Papa this weekend. Any plans?"

"Yeah, Aunt Marie is coming up from Portland this weekend, so we get to hang out with our cousins," London says bouncing around the room. I'm grateful Eva has a large family who are all relatively close to the Seattle area. Being an only child on my side creates a small family.

"You girls have fun. I will see you Sunday night and I love you to the moon and back."

"Love you, too," they say before ending the call.

Early the next morning, I'm awoken by a soft knock on my door. Looking through the peephole I see my best friend with two coffees in her hands.

"Took you long enough," she says pushing her way into my room as soon as I open the door.

"Well, yeah. It's only seven thirty in the morning. What did you expect?"

"Not to be standing out here so long," Nicolette teases.

"Sorry my sleeping inconvenienced you, shorty." I throw on a T-shirt and eagerly take the coffee she brought. "You ready for tonight?"

"Yes. No. I think so." She puts her head in her hands and won't look up at me.

"What's wrong, Nic?"

"What if I'm making a mistake? What if Brad isn't the one? What if we end up divorced, like you and Eva?"

"Gee, thanks. You'll be fine. You're just getting cold feet."

"But what if it's not? What if…" She stops mid-sentence.

"What?" I ask.

Nicolette comes and sits next to me on the bed. "What if it's supposed to be us?"

What the fuck? Really?

"I haven't been able to stop thinking about you for the last few weeks. We have been together our entire lives. Maybe we're supposed to be together," she says, quietly.

"Nicolette, you know it's not supposed to be us. I'm sorry for ever questioning our relationship. You and Brad are meant to be together."

"Do you really believe we are?"

"If I didn't, I wouldn't be here." Plus, I'd be an asshole if I said anything different.

"Thank you."

"That's what best friends are for. Now, you go off and get all gorgeous and I will see you tonight."

"Thanks again, Connor." Nicolette reaches up on her tiptoes and kisses me.

Fuck me. Where's my fucking whiskey?

Teri Kay

CHAPTER FOUR

Daniella

"**A**RE YOU SURE YOU** want to watch Aaron this weekend?" I ask my sister-in-law, Leilani.

"Why wouldn't I?"

"Because you're only visiting for a few weeks. The last thing I want to do is tie you down with a six-year-old for the weekend."

"Spending the weekend with my nephew is not being tied down," she retorts.

"Maybe I shouldn't go," I debate.

"You're going away with your friend for the weekend. Aaron and I will be just fine."

"Thank you. I kinda need this," I say sheepishly. I don't want to admit to Leilani I'm lonely. I still love her brother so much and I don't want his family to ever feel like I'm betraying his memory.

"Makoa would want you to find happiness again," she says as if she's just read my mind.

"I know, but it brings an overwhelming sense of guilt. Mak held my heart."

"We know. But now we're worried about you."

"We?" I question. "Who's we?"

"Mama and Papa. They worry about you, Daniella. You're like a daughter to them."

Hearing her say that makes my eyes swell with tears. The fact Makoa's parents still think of me as their daughter when my own parents didn't even want me, blows me away. My father walked out on my mother when I was two and caring for me by herself was too difficult, so she left me with my grandmother. I haven't spoken to my mother since my grandmother's funeral over a decade ago. I prefer to keep her out of my life.

"Makoa is your guardian angel now. He is watching over you and Aaron. One day, you will be together again, but hopefully many, many years from now. Too long to be alone. You need to find happiness again to give your boy the happy life he deserves," Leilani continues.

"Thank you. I needed to hear that. Your family is my only family and I don't want to lose you guys.

"You never will." She pulls me into a hug letting me know everything will be just fine.

"Mom! Auntie Addy is here!" Aaron shouts from the front room.

"Thanks, little man. I'll be right there. Ok, my flight and hotel information are on the fridge. I'll keep my cell on me at all times in case you need anything."

"Daniella, stop. We'll be just fine. You don't need to worry."

"I know. Thank you. Alright, I'm outta here. See you guys Sunday night."

I give Aaron a huge hug and kiss before Addyson and I take off for her cousin's wedding in Spokane this weekend.

Having one too many glasses of wine between the airport and the plane, makes the Uber ride to the hotel an interesting adventure. Luckily, Addy had pre-booked everything, so the poor guy knew exactly where to take us. Otherwise who knows where we would have ended up.

"Thanks for coming with me this weekend," she says.

"Of course. I'm happy to replace Josh anytime." We both laugh. "Why couldn't he come?"

"The wedding was planned only a month ago and he already had plans with his brother to go fishing. My mom thinks the bride is knocked up."

"What an awful thing to say. Why would she think she's pregnant?"

"'Cause she's a bitter old woman," Addy jokes. "Plus, Brad and this chick have only known each other like six months."

"Just watch and see if she drinks tomorrow," I suggest.

"Nope. I'm gonna be scoping out the guys."

"Again, fiancé at home."

"Not for me. For you."

"Ha! Whatever. C'mon, let's get some sleep. I'm beat."

ADDYSON WENT TO THE venue earlier in the day to assist her aunt and mother in setting up the reception area. She invited me along with her, but rarely do I get time to myself anymore, so I opted to stay behind and take advantage of the spa the hotel offers.

Leilani's words keep ringing in my ears preventing me from relaxing during this incredible massage. Is it ok to move on? I still love Makoa with all my heart. Why would another man want to share my heart with him? Would Aaron think I'm trying to replace his dad?

I push all thoughts of Makoa and Aaron out of my mind. As selfish as that might be, I want to make this weekend about me.

After falling asleep on the massage table, I enter the sauna to wake up my skin and my mind. As much as I try and avoid it, my mind keeps drifting back to my sister-in-law's words telling me I need to find happiness again, for Aaron and myself.

Addyson has hooked me up with one of those stylist-by-mail deals and at first, I was a bit skeptical. I have curves. My son gave me my hips and boobs, and the amazing food of the islands gave me a tummy. I have a tough time finding clothes to make me feel sexy. Yet, Dina, the by mail stylist, has done it.

Slipping the stunning maxi dress over my body I step back to examine myself in the mirror. Flowers in shades of pink, seafoam green, and yellow ripple across a black chiffon dress as it shapes a surplice bodice allowing my breasts to peak out just enough to be sexy. The billowing ankle length skirt has a front slit, which shows off my remaining Hawaiian tan and falls just below the elasticized waist for a stunning finish. I've chosen a pair of rose-colored suede lace-up heels and a gold choker chain to complete the look.

"Holy shit," I whisper to myself. It's been a long time since I've looked this hot. "Who knows maybe I'll meet a good-looking guy tonight."

Grabbing my purse, I join the other guests who are waiting for the arranged shuttle to take us to the McAllister Farm, where the wedding is being held.

The venue is stunning. I've always been obsessed with outdoor weddings, especially ones with a rustic barn, like this location. The McAllister Farm is a sprawling piece of land, nestled in the Washington foothills. The property has two fully restored barns, several small ponds, a quaint little bed and breakfast, and trees which have stood for over one hundred years.

I send Addyson a text to let her know I'm here. She tells me to grab our seats toward the middle of the groom's side and she'll meet me in ten minutes. In no rush, I make my way along the pathway to the ceremony area. I find myself lost in the beauty of the old willow trees and the bright colors of the new spring flowers.

My thoughts are broken by a voice off in the distance. Where the hell have I heard that voice before? I strain to try and see who it's come from, but my view is blocked by the ample trees.

"I thought you were going to get us seats?" Addyson asks, startling me from behind.

"Sorry, got distracted by these amazing willow trees." I shrug with no other reasonable excuse.

"I've got to tell you—"

"Ladies and gentlemen. Can everyone kindly make their way to their seats? The ceremony is about to begin," the D.J. says interrupting Addy.

"C'mon. If we're late, I'll never hear the end of it from my mother," she says. She takes my hand and pulls me up the softly lit walkway to our seats.

The altar is in front of one of the older barns. A canopy ceiling of lace and white lights perfectly adorned with bright yellow daisies covers the guest seating area. With the sunlight dimming at dusk, the entire setting has a heartening amber glow.

As the wedding party gathers in an area behind the guests, I happen to catch one of the guys sneak a swig from a flask he's attempting to hide in his jacket.

"Ha! Is the groom so nervous he has to sneak shots?" I joke.

"What are you talking about? Brad's up front talking to the minister," Addy informs me.

"Oh shit. Then who's the guy sneaking shots?"

"Do you need glasses?" she asks, with a sneaky smile.

"Addy, what's going on?"

Our conversation is cut short when a beautiful instrumental version of *A Thousand Years* by Christina Perri begins to play. The wedding party is small, with just the bride's maid of honor and Brad's best man. When the bride approaches the aisle runner, I can see why Addy's cousin snatched her up so quickly. Nicolette is gorgeous. Tall, blonde and skinny. The three things women aspire to be.

"She's so tall," I whisper.

"Nope. Six-inch stiletto heels. I guess she hates being short."

Nicolette's father is pushed up next to her in a wheelchair. Yet, that's not what catches me off guard. The fact Connor Evans, aka Karaoke Connor, aka Mr. Rude is pushing his wheelchair, is what practically knocks me off my seat.

"What the hell?" I mouth to Addyson.

"I'll explain later," she says.

Connor keeps his head down, almost as if he doesn't want to be here. But when he turns to sit down, our eyes lock. His intense blue eyes flash me a look of shock sending a shiver down my spine.

As soon as the ceremony is over, I pull Addyson to the side. "What the hell is Connor doing here?"

"Apparently he and the bride have been best friends since birth."

"Huh? Ok. I wonder why he was throwing back shots before the ceremony?"

"I don't know. Maybe you should talk to him since the universe keeps bringing you two together."

"Mr. Rude? Yeah, right!"

"Who knows? Maybe the third time's the charm." She giggles. "C'mon. Let's get to the reception while there's still money on the open bar."

Four gin and tonics later, Addy and I are the life of the dance floor. I'm not usually the one to be overly outgoing or to let my hair down, but tonight, with my best friend, I feel safe and free. Coincidently, I've noticed Connor's absence for most of the reception. He shows up just as something important happens and then disappears just as quick.

"Everyone having a good time?" the DJ asks the crowd. The guests erupt in cheers. "We have a special treat for you all tonight. I have been told Connor, the bride's best friend, is an incredible singer and has prepared something special for our lovely couple."

Connor approaches the stage, taking the microphone from the DJ. The sunken shoulders, deep set eyes, and shaky hands give a much different persona than the cocky ass I met at Slick's. He seems quite uncomfortable with the situation.

"Nicolette, you look stunning tonight. Brad brings out a sparkle in your eyes, I've yet to see before. You have been my best friend since the day you were born and now it's time for me to hand those reins over to your new best friend. Take care of her, man."

He points to the DJ and the music starts. Immediately, I recognize the sounds of Billy Joel's piano. My grandmother and I would listen to his music for hours together when I was growing up. *She's Got a Way* was our favorite song. Why does Connor keep choosing these songs I have deep connections to?

As Connor continues with his song, he watches Nicolette dance with her husband as I watch him. Each time the friends are face to face, their eyes connect. Until he sees me and for a few brief moments, when his eyes meet mine, it feels like we are the only two people in the room. My hands start to sweat, my heart is practically jumping out of my chest, and I can feel my nipples pebble under the sheer material of this dress. This man's voice is intoxicating.

As quickly as the song started, it ends, and Connor has once again taken off.

"Did you see where Connor went?" I ask Addy. "Thought maybe I'd ask him to dance before the night is over."

"I think he's outside on the patio. Go find him. I'll meet you back at the hotel, I've got to help my mother with some clean up shit anyways."

"Sounds good."

"Don't do anything I wouldn't do," Addyson teases.

"Whatever."

Stepping through the double glass doors, the frosty night air bites, causing goosebumps to sting my skin. Even though it's early spring, the nights in Washington are much colder than in Hawaii and I'm still not quite used to the weather here.

I don't see Conner on the patio. Maybe I'll walk around the grounds a bit and see if we bump into each other. If not, it wasn't meant to be and I'm just going to head back to the hotel and call it a night.

Rounding the corner, I hear the muffled voices of two people arguing. Not wanting to intrude, I turn around to leave, until one of the voices becomes recognizably clear and I'm frozen in place.

"Are you fucking kidding me, Nicolette?" Connor shouts at the new bride.

"Shhh! Connor be quiet and do not yell at me like that."

"What the fuck ever, Nic. We're supposed to be best friends. First you keep Brad a secret from me and now this. Friends don't lie to each other."

Ouch! Even though I don't know him at all, I can hear the hurt in Connor's voice.

"I didn't lie to you Connor. I just didn't tell anyone. I haven't even told Brad."

"Why the fuck did you kiss me this morning?"

"I don't know," Nicolette says meekly.

"Bullshit!" Connor yells.

Ok, none of my business, but no bride should have to be treated like this on her wedding day. Let's see if I remember any of my crappy acting skills I learned back in high school drama class.

"There you are. I've been looking for you all over," I say approaching the arguing friends. Both stare at me dumbfounded, neither one really recognizing who I am.

"Me?" they question in unison.

"Connor, don't you remember asking me to save you a dance this evening. Reception's almost over and I would really like to dance."

"I'm sorry, you are?" Nicolette asks with a noticeable irritation in her voice.

"Daniella Kahele. I am here as the guest of Addyson Baker, Brad's cousin."

"London and Daniella's son, Aaron, are also in the same kindergarten class," Connor explains.

"Nici!" I hear a man's voice, which I can only assume to be Brad's shouting from the patio.

"I need to go," she says.

"Congratulations. Have a great night," I say as she rushes up to her new groom.

"What the hell was that all about?" Connor questions me.

"Whatever is going on between you and the bride is none of my business, but no woman deserves to be treated like that on her wedding day. Especially, by her best friend. You'll thank me later."

"Doubt it," he grumbles just loud enough for me to hear. I can't help but giggle at the grouchy pants he's being. Oh my god — Did I just call him grouchy pants? I really need to start having more adult conversations. The thought of this makes me laugh even harder.

"Something funny?" he asks.

"I was just thinking I need to have more adult conversations."

"Yeah, why is that?"

"'Cause in my head I called you a grouchy pants." Saying it out loud, it sounds even funnier than in my head.

"Ha! That's what London calls me."

"Smart kid." The smile sneaking across his lips lets me know he can take my subtle teasing.

Now that my buzz has worn off, I don't have the courage to ask Connor to dance for real this time. "Well, goodnight." Like an idiot, I turn and start to walk back up to the patio.

"Daniella!" I turn around and Connor is only two feet behind me.

"Damn you're quick," I tease.

"For a big guy, I do have some speed. Baseball."

"Oh, cool."

"So," he stammers, shuffling his feet. "Did you wanna dance?"

"Honestly, my buzz is starting to wear off and these shoes are killing my feet. I think I may head back to my hotel and grab a drink there." Here goes nothing. "Would you like to join me?"

"You know what? I would love to. Let's get the hell out of here." Connor places his hand on the small of my back and guides me to the cars waiting to take guests home.

"Conner!"

"Wait here, ok?"

"I'll grab us a car," I suggest.

"Thank you."

"Told you you'd thank me later." I laugh.

It's Nicolette calling him over. It's obvious she's irritated he was planning on leaving without saying goodbye to her or her family. He gives each one of them a quick hug and then quickly jogs back to jump in our car.

"Ready?" I ask.

"Let's get the hell out of here," Connor tells the driver.

Sensing Connor needs a few moments to calm down again after his interaction with Nicolette, I don't attempt to initiate any conversation. Instead, I grab my phone to see if I have any missed messages. Leilani has sent me the most adorable picture of Aaron and her tucked in bed together eating popcorn. As much as I miss my little man, I'm enjoying my weekend away.

"Text from home?" he asks.

"Yeah." I show him my phone. "Aaron and my sister-in-law. Where is London this weekend?"

"Her and her sister are staying with my ex-wife's family."

"Do you miss them?" I ask.

"My ex-wife's family? Not one little bit," he jokes.

"I meant your kids?"

"Here we are folks," the driver interrupts us.

"Well this is convenient," Connor says.

"What is?"

"Us staying at the same hotel."

Immediately, I squint my eyes, giving him my I don't think so look.

"I just meant I don't have to find a ride somewhere else. I can stumble back to my room here."

"Do you drink a lot?" I ask.

"No. I know it may seem like I do from the few times we've met, but I don't. I'm raising my daughters practically on my own, so there aren't many opportunities for drinking."

"Wait? I thought you said you have an ex-wife."
"I do. Why don't we go get out of these fancy wedding digs and meet back down here in twenty minutes, and I'll tell you about my crazy situation."

"Sounds good to me."

Slipping out of my dress and into my jeans feels a thousand times more comfortable. I'm a low maintenance girl, heels and dresses usually aren't my thing. Honestly, I'd love to throw on my bathing suit and go soak in the hot tub for a while. I have no idea if Connor would be down for something like that.

The hotel phone startles me from my dilemma. "Hello?"

"Daniella?"

"Yes."

"Hey. It's Connor. I was wondering if you'd wanna hit up the hot tub instead of the bar? If not, it's cool," he stammers over his own words.

"You read my mind."

"I'll grab us some drinks and meet you there in ten."

So, when I said I wanted to let my hair down with someone, I never expected it to be Connor Evans. But maybe Mr. Rude won't be bad after all.

Teri Kay

Conner

CHAPTER FIVE

"A Twist in My Story"

W HAT THE HELL ARE the odds Daniella Kahele would be at Nicolette's wedding and now sharing a hot tub and a drink with me. Even though I do find her extremely attractive, I need to remind myself she's off limits.

Maybe asking a sexy married woman to join me in the hot tub wasn't the best idea I've had tonight, but it isn't my worst. Yet, stepping into another man's territory is a line I won't cross.

"Hey," Daniella says shyly, entering the hotel's pool area.

"Hi. Your feet feel better?" This makes her laugh. Damn, her smile is gorgeous.

"Much. Thank you. You seriously read my mind when you called. Such a better idea than the bar."

"I thought so too. I grabbed us a couple beers since we can't have glass in this area."

"Perfect."

"You ready to get in?" I ask, pulling my shirt over my head.

"Sure." Daniella throws her towel on a chair and makes her way into the scalding water, one toe at a time.

"Wait. Aren't you forgetting something?" I ask.

"Umm. No, I don't think so?"

"Why are you still wearing your little dress thingy?"

"You mean my cover-up?"

"Is that what those things are called? I need to remember to get a few of those for my daughter this summer. In black. Knee length and long sleeves." I laugh.

"This stays on," she explains.

"Why?" I scrunch my forehead in confusion.

"Because of all the extra little gifts my son left me when he was born." Daniella opts to stay on the side of the hot tub dangling her feet in the water.

"Curves on a woman are sexy as fuck. Hell, curves on anyone are sexy." I stand up and rub my oversized belly. I know I'm a bigger guy, but I love food, and more importantly I love myself.

Her cheeks turn a bright shade of red, which I'm not sure is from what I said or the heat coming from the water. "Well, as cute as they are on you, mine will stay under the cover-up."

"Your husband isn't going to come and kick my ass for calling you sexy, is he?" I tease.

"Excuse me?" In one quick instant, all the color drained from her face, leaving her pale as a ghost.

"You wear a wedding ring, so I assumed you are married. Daniella, are you ok? I hope I didn't upset you."

"It's ok. Honestly, I've been thinking about not wearing it anymore," she says sadly.

I move myself next to her feet which are still gently swaying in the water. "Wanna talk about it?"

"Not really. Can I just give you the condensed version tonight?"

"You can give me anything you want, sweetheart."

"I was married. My husband died in a military helicopter crash just over a year ago. Now it's just me and my little man."

"Can I ask you a question?"

"Sure."

"Why are you thinking about taking it off?" I ask.

"Because I need to find my happy place again. I think I may want to start dating." Hearing her say this causes my heart to ache and my dick to twitch simultaneously. Sometimes, being a guy is a shitty thing.

"You deserve to be happy Daniella. I'm sure your husband wants happiness for you. And any guy who doesn't understand why you still wear his ring doesn't deserve you."

"Thank you, Connor. So, now tell me about this ex-wife of yours."

"Ugh! Do I have to?"

"Yup. I told you my sob story, now you tell me yours."

"Let's see. I married my high school sweetheart. We had kids young, but Eva wasn't the 'stay at home and raise kids' type of person. So, she joined the military, and I did freelance sports writing. Until about a year ago, when she decided she is a lesbian and fell in love with her secretary, Heather."

"Crazy. So why are you doing this by yourself? You should have two moms helping you."

"Eva is computer genius and works in the cyberterrorism division of the army. She is on a lengthy, secret mission in Thailand somewhere. The girls didn't want to move to Asia, so instead, I bought a house in Redmond and became a single dad of two amazing girls."

"No way!" she shouts.

"What?" I can't help but laugh at her excitement.

"I bought a house in Redmond a few months ago. I'm in the Northern Lights neighborhood."

"No shit. I live across the street in the Blue Dream homes back up against the woods. What a small fucking world. I think we're meant to be friends Ms. Daniella."

"And why is that?"

"We both like karaoke, even though I am much better than you," I tease.

"I won't deny that, Karaoke Conner. I don't know if just liking karaoke is a reason for us to be friends." I love how she can handle me being a smartass and then throws it right back at me.

"Let me continue. Our kids are in the same class, so it's always nice to have a friendly face at those horrible singing performances they make us sit through."

"Oh my god! What a horrible thing to say about those little sweethearts."

"Oh, they may be sweet, but you know not one of them can sing a lick."

"They can be pretty bad sometimes," she admits.

"And now that I know we live close, we can be dog walking buddies," I say. My enthusiasm about dog walking makes her giggle.

"We don't have a dog," Daniella says.

"I think you should change that. Every boy needs a dog. And plus, I need a dog walking buddy."

"Something to look into. I mean for Aaron and all. So, care to share what had your panties all knotted up with the bride tonight?"

"Not particularly, but I will, but only if you take off your silly cover-up and get in this hot tub with me."

"Fine Mr. Pushy. You win." Daniella stands and lifts the dress up over her head. Extra gifts my ass. This girl has perfect curves in all the right places. She sits down next to me in the hot tub, her leg gently brushes against mine. Thank god for the jets and bubbles or my raging hard-on may have become our next topic of conversation.

"First of all, thank you for not letting me make a bigger ass of myself than I already was. I noticed early in the day Nicolette was sticking to water. At first, I didn't think much of. I just assumed she didn't want to be plastered walking down the aisle. I confronted her on it and she told me she's late and thinks she might be pregnant."

"Holy Shit! I gotta ask, cause I'm nosy. I heard you say she kissed you?"

"Yup. In my hotel. Nicolette and I have always been best friends. We both had those 'what if' moments recently. But now she's Mrs. Brad Langley and those moments have passed."

"Wow. I'm sorry."

"Don't be. Must mean something better is on my horizon."

"Have you dated much since your divorce?" she asks.

"Not much. I did a little before Eva moved to Thailand. Now, I'm learning how to raise two daughters on my own, so my time is limited. And the few women I have been set up with are either not what I'm looking for or are just bat shit fucking crazy."

"Oh, they couldn't have been that bad," Daniella says pushing on my arm.

"I'm stuck in this in-between dating age, where women either want to stay out and drink until four a.m. or they sit and tap their watch because their biological clock is ticking. I actually had a woman tell me she would be able to clean me up before our kids are born."

"Holy shit! Really? How many times had you guys gone out?"

"It was out first date."

"See, it's this type of shit that makes me fearful of dating again," Daniella says as she takes another swig off her beer. Damn, her lips are gorgeous. Is it bad I'm already picturing them wrapped around my dick. "Especially, at my age." Her comment breaks my concentration on her lips.

"I'm sure a gorgeous woman like you in her twenties is going to have no problem dating in a town like Seattle."

"Thank you for the compliment, but I wish I was still in my twenties. I'm thirty-three."

"Oh, an older woman," I tease her.

"How old are you, mister?" she asks.

"Thirty-one."

"And your oldest is?"

"Just turned twelve. Senior prom baby."

"Interesting." She giggles.

"The pool is closing in ten minutes, folks," the attendant informs us.

"Damn, that sucks. I was enjoying my evening talking to you," she says getting out of the hot tub and grabbing the towel she threw on the chair.

"Well, I have a few more beers in my room. Want to help me finish them off before we call it a night?"

Her eyes close briefly as she contemplates her answer. I use this small second of time to hop out and bring my body next to hers. I'm drawn to everything about this woman; her long, thick, blonde hair, amazing silver-blue eyes, and these hips I can't wait to grab onto.

"Hey." I put my finger under her chin and lift her eyes to meet mine. "It's just a few beers and some friendly conversation. Nothing more, sweetheart." But fuck I know I already want more. So much more.

"Sounds perfect," she whispers softly.

"Good." I lace my hand in hers and we make our way to the elevator.

We stop by Daniella's room, so she can change, let Addyson know where she'll be, and then head up two more floors to my room. While I change, Daniella makes herself at home grabbing us beers and finding some music to put on. I come out of the bathroom to find her propped up with all the pillows against the headboard of my bed.

"So, tell me Connor. If you're not looking for the party all night girl or the one's whose clocks are beating down your door, who are you looking for?"

"I don't know. I guess someone down the middle. A woman who wants to go out and have an enjoyable time but understands I have two little girls who I like to do things with on the weekends."

"Sounds like what Makoa and I used to do with Aaron whenever he wasn't overseas," she says quietly.

"I'm sorry, Daniella. I didn't mean to upset you."

"You didn't. I will forever miss my husband, but I know he isn't coming back. I hope someday I will meet someone who can accept me and my son with the love I still have in my heart for him."

Me! Me! Me! I silently scream in my head, but there's no way in hell I'll allow those words to come out of my mouth.

"Any man would be lucky to have you and Aaron in his life, Daniella." For whatever reason this statement makes her giggle.

"Did I say something funny?"

"You say my name a lot."

"I do?" Shit, she noticed.

"Are you like forgetful or something? Such the hottie player you have to constantly remind yourself which girl you're with?" she sasses me.

"Damn, you caught me. This dad bod has girls lining up around the corner."

"It's not the dad bod, it's those damn striking blue eyes," she says quickly throwing her hands up over her mouth like those words weren't supposed to slip out.

"So, you like my eyes?" I ask scooting my body next to hers.

"They're not bad. But stop changing the subject and answer my question." It's so cute watching her try to get stern with me without laughing.

"And what question might that be, Ms. Daniella?"

"That! Right there! What is the deal with saying my name?"

84

"I find women whose names end in an 'a' very sexy."

"Really?"

"Hey, I have the eyes; you have the name. I think we're destined, sweetheart."

"I think we might be," Daniella says with a blushing smile. "Walk me back to my room?"

"Of course."

IT'S BEEN A WEEK since the wedding, and I can't seem to get Daniella Kahele out of my every waking thought. I was hoping to see her at school, but I learned Aaron is dropped off and picked up by a babysitter. And with all the conversations had last weekend, we never did talk about work.

Breaking me out of my Daniella haze, Colton sends me a text.

Colton- Hey man, what are you up to tonight?

Me- My guess is I'll be knee deep in glitter and unicorns by seven. Why?

Colton- Dude, that's just wrong.

Me- Life of a dad. You'll see one day.

Colton- I have a date tonight with a smoking hot chick I met the other night. She wants to bring her sister along. I need a wingman.

Me- I don't know. I was away last weekend and I don't have anyone to watch the girls.

Colton- Is this about the curvy blonde?

Me- No, it's about my kids.

As if their ears were burning, Harper and London run into the room. "Dad!" they shout simultaneously.

"What? What's on fire? Who's dead? More importantly, where did you hide the body?" I tease.

"Daddy!" London giggles and jumps into my lap. "We hid the body in the attic, but—" she puts her finger over her lip and makes a Shh sound, "don't tell anyone our secret."

"Remind me to stop letting you watch the scary movies with me. Now, what's up ladies?"

"Cassie and her little sister Maggie have invited us over for a slumber party tonight. Their cousins are visiting and they want us to come over also. Do you think we can go?" Harper asks.

Holy shit, the timing on this couldn't be more perfect. "Let me clear it with Mrs. Fletcher, but I don't have a problem with it."

"Woo-hoo!" London shouts fist pumping the air.

"Wow. Are you that excited to get away from me?" I ask.

"No, Daddy, but Mrs. Fletcher knows how to braid my hair pretty," my youngest daughter says. It breaks my heart her mother chooses her career over moments like these.

"Go pack. I'll call Mrs. Fletcher now."

Me- I'm in.

Colton- Awesome. We can bring along glitter and unicorns if you want man?

Me- Hey, whatever floats your boat. Text me the details. I'll see you tonight.

Colton- Meet at the needle at 7

Me- Really? The needle?

Colton- She's from out of town and wants to go. Suck it up buttercup and do this for me cause this chick is fucking hot.

Me- Mine or yours?

Colton- If her sister looks anything like her, you're in for a fucking treat dude. See you tonight.

The Fletcher family has been wonderful to my girls since we moved into the neighborhood earlier this year. She has been a savior in those last minute little girl crises I just can't seem to pull together. Mainly hair. And bras. Oh my god, there is nothing worse than shopping for a bra with a twelve-year-old girl.

After walking the girls across the street, I decide to check my emails before jumping in the shower to get ready for the 'oh so fun' blind-wingman date. Scrolling through, it's all the same shit. Bills, junk, buy this, bills, sell that, and always more bills. And then I see it. An email from HawaiiMom519@email.com. Really? On the night I'm supposed to go out with fucking Colton, I get an email from the woman I've been dreaming about all week.

Teri Kay

To: BigDaddyof2Ladies@email.com
From: HawaiiMom519@email.com

Hi Connor,
Hope it's ok I got your email off the school list. Had a wonderful time last weekend. Maybe soon I can repay you for those beers? And I may need some advice on what kind of dog to get. Will I see you at the Spring Carnival next weekend? Have a good weekend.
Daniella

Even though I'm running short on time, I will not let this email go without a reply. Something about this woman keeps drawing me in. I want to know more about her. Yet, I'm afraid if I push her too fast, she may not be ready.

To: HawaiiMom519@email.com
From: BigDaddyof2Ladies@email.com

Hey Daniella,
Stalking me now, are you? I love it. I'll definitely take you up on those beers. I will be going to the Carnival. Somehow, I got volunteered for the dunk tank. I know the perfect place to help you decide the kind of dog you and Aaron would like. Maybe you can go with London and I this week.
Enjoy your weekend also, sweetheart.
Connor

Only having an hour until I need to meet Colton and his ladies, I take a quick shower, shave and make myself look presentable. I don't go out of my way to look overly handsome, since nine times out of ten Colton goes home with both ladies and I go home by myself. Ok, so it's only happened twice, but who's counting.

Colton is a handsome man, undeniably. Even though he's a short fucker, ladies love those bulging muscles and the killer, sparkly smile. He was even approached recently by a local photographer to do some modeling for her. And then you have me; the large guy with the gorgeous eyes and amazing sense of humor who makes them all laugh, but no one wants to date.

As much as I'm not wanting to do this, the bro-code says I must go and be the best wingman I can be. I would much rather be taking Daniella up on those beers tonight.

Teri Kay

CHAPTER SIX

Daniella

"LEILANI, I REALLY DON'T want to go out tonight. It's been a rough week at work and I just want to crawl up in bed with Aaron and relax."

"Did you forget Aaron's not here?"

"Oh shit, that's right. He's spending the night at his friend Kevin's house. So, let's stay in and just drink a whole bottle of wine and watch Fifty Shades."

"Nope, I have a date with a hot guy and I don't want to go alone," she says.

"Awesome, so I'm the third wheel. No thank you," I huff.

"Well, not exactly."

"What did you do?"

"I told him I wouldn't go unless my sister could go with me and he said he had a buddy who would be perfect."

"Perfect? Two strangers go out with two strangers? How would he know he has a perfect buddy?"

"I don't know. But c'mon Dani please. What would momma and papa think if they found out you let their baby girl go out with a strange man all by herself?"

"Oh! Not fair! Fine! But I won't enjoy myself," I tease.

"You could at least give him a chance," Leilani suggests.

"We'll see."

Ever since the wedding and our night in the hot tub, Connor Evans and his crystal-blue eyes have invaded my brain. The conversations we had that night made me feel more relaxed than I have in months. Yet, I also sense he's ready for a serious relationship and I don't think I can make that kind of commitment yet.

On Wednesday, I sent him a simple email, but have yet to hear back. I figure he's just busy with work and his kids. Or maybe I read the whole situation wrong and he really wasn't interested in me.

Throwing on a pair of black skinny jeans and a bright purple sweater I bought last week, I give myself a once over in my closet mirror. I put my long golden tresses back in a ponytail, dab a small amount of makeup on my face and holler to Leilani, "I'll be ready to go in ten minutes."

Never in a million years did I think I would find myself in this position again. I hated the whole dating thing in my teens, found the man of my dreams in my twenties, and here I am in my thirties starting over. I'd much rather be snuggled up with Connor on a couch somewhere sharing those beers I owe him.

"Ride's here!" My sister-in-law shouts from the other room.

The Uber driver is hot. He stands there waiting for us, holding the door open and both Leilani and I giggle like little school girls.

"Good evening ladies. My name is Jamal, I'll be taking you to the Space Needle tonight. With traffic, the drive should take about forty minutes."

"The Needle?" I ask.

"C'mon, I've never been there. Remember when you first moved to Hawaii? I had to take you to every damn place you ever saw in a movie."

"Fine. Fine." I laugh.

"Hot dates, ladies?" Jamal asks.

"Apparently, hers is. I'm just a wingman."

"A lady as fine as yourself will never be *just* a wingman." I can feel my cheeks heat from the smoothness in his voice.

"This date is just as much for her as it is for me," Leilani chimes in.

"Well, I hope you both have a fun time."

"So, who's this guy you're meeting?"

"His name is Colton. I met him at Slick's last week."

"Oh. My. God. Seriously? The bouncer?" I ask.

"What? Do you know him?"

"No, not really. Addyson called him sex on stick a few weeks ago. Not my type. Too much muscle for me. Girl, he sang *Save a Horse Ride a Cowboy* during karaoke night." I hear Jamal chuckle from the front seat.

"He is damn sexy," she says.

"He better not have brought one of his gym rat buddies."

"We're here ladies." Jamal comes around to open our door. "Please call me if your date turns out to be an over-muscled gym rat." He hands me his card, gets back in his car and takes off down the street.

"Colton just sent me a text saying he and his buddy are waiting for us in the restaurant on the observation deck."

"Here goes nothing," I whisper under my breath.

The entire ride up the elevator, I'm questioning why I let Leilani talk me into this. I'm awful at making small talk. I just come off as shy and awkward. But you know what, this isn't about me. Leilani is the closest person I'll ever have to a sister and I would be devastated if anything ever happened to her.

"I'm so excited." Leilani bounces up and down before the doors open.

"Stop, girl. You look desperate."

"Whatever! I only have another week before I head home and I plan on getting all the man meat I can."

"Oh my god. Please don't ever say that again."

"What? Man meat?"

"C'mon, you have to admit Colton is one fine ass piece of meat."

"Typical woman. Only wanting me for my body. I do have a brain, ya know," Colton teases. Leilani and I were laughing so hard over her man meat comment that we failed to notice the elevator doors had opened and there he stood waiting for us.

"Maybe, but I'm only in town long enough to care about your body," she teases back.

"Leilani!" I give her a motherly smack on the arm.

"What? It's true. Colton, this is my sister—"

"Feisty Blonde. I remember you," he interrupts her.

"That would be me."

"Damn, Connor's gonna shit," Colton says with a mischievous laugh.

"Now what could possibly make me shit on a first date?" a voice from behind me chimes into our conversation; a voice I haven't been able to get out of my head for the past week. The smell of cigarettes and Acqua Di Gio overwhelm each sense in my body causing me to have to fight the weakness in my knees.

"Me," I say, turning around to see the striking blue eyes of Conner Evans.

"Yup, that would do it," he says with a priceless look of shock on his face. "What are you doing here?"

"Yes, Connor, it's good to see you too," I say throwing out a sarcastic attitude. "And I was invited by my sister."

"You're my blind date?"

"He's not too bright, is he?" Leilani leans over and whispers in my ear.

"Doesn't seem to be." I can't help but let a sneaky smile creep over my face.

"Knox, party of four. Knox." The host calls us and leads us to our table.

Throughout dinner, I catch Connor glancing in my direction when he thinks I'm not looking. Being the mother of a five-year-old little boy, I have learned to see everything. Or maybe I catch him because I'm also stealing sexy little glances.

Connor Evans is hard to read. After my first impression, I wanted nothing to do with Mr. Rude, but then watching him with London at school showed me a softer side. Even though he seemed attracted to me last weekend, he never kissed me, he never made a move besides briefly holding my hand or even asked for my number.

"Have you been to the Space Needle before?" Connor asks startling me out of my lost train of thoughts.

"Only once. The guy I was dating before I moved to Hawaii was deathly afraid of heights. It limited our dates to nothing further than six feet off the ground. He said anything taller than him was a splatter waiting to happen."

"What an oddly fascinating theory."

"No, it was stupid." I laugh.

"Wanna get out of here?" Connor asks.

"Well, then we wouldn't be good wingmen, now would we?"

"I think they will be just fine." He points to Leilani and Colton, who have started making out in the booth across from us.

"Leilani? Will you be ok if I go?" I ask already knowing the answer. She shoos me away without ever removing her lips from Colton's.

"C'mon," Connor says grabbing my hand and pulling me to the elevator.

As the doors shut, I realize we didn't pay for our dinners. "Shit, Connor. We have to go back. We left without paying."

"No, we don't. They asked us to dinner. They can pay." I'll have to remind myself to pay Leilani back when she gets home.

"Is there anything you'd like to do?" Connor asks as he hails a taxi.

"Get to know you a little better," I say shyly.

"I think I know the perfect place."

When the taxi starts making its way toward the water, I have a pretty good idea of where our destination may be. Aaron is going to be so disappointed I did this without him.

"What's wrong?" he asks.

"Nothing. Just thinking about Aaron."

"Everything ok with him?"

"Perfect."

"He looks a lot like your sister," Connor comments.

"Yeah. They both are dead ringers for Makoa."

Even in the dim light of the taxi cab, I see confusion cloud Connor's eyes. "Leilani is Mak's little sister. Ever since we met, she has always called me her sister, never her sister-in-law. Not having any siblings, I loved finally having a sister."

"Here we are folks. Enjoy the rest of your night." Stepping out of the cab, I see my suspicions were correct.

"The Ferris wheel, huh?"

"Ever ridden it before?"

"Nope. I've been promising Aaron I'd take him here for a while now."

"We'll take him during the day, but it's a whole other experience at night." The way he says "we'll" makes me smile. The fact Connor wants to do things with Aaron has me floating a bit right now.

Connor links his fingers in mine as we make our way through the park to the ride. Standing in line to buy tickets, I start thinking about the irony and coincidences of the evening. Maybe Addy is right and the world is trying to bring us together.

"What are you thinking about?" he asks.

"Isn't that supposed to be the chicks line?" I retort.

"Hey, I'm a curious guy." I can feel my cheeks turn red again. "Oh, don't get all shy on me now, sweetheart."

"As I was getting ready tonight, I was thinking how I'd rather be hanging out with you than going out on a set up date."

"See I told you. Destined."

"What?" I ask, laughing.

"I was thinking the exact same thing. And I will gladly take you up on those beers any day."

"So, you did get my email?"

"Right before I started getting ready tonight. Wanna know a secret?" Connor whispers.

"What?"

"I only made myself presentable tonight," he jokes, sliding his hands down his sides and doing a silly little model turn.

"What are you talking about?" I literally think my smile is reaching from ear to ear.

"So, after Colton called me and asked me to be his wingman for his date's sister, I checked my email and from then on I was doomed."

"And why was that?" I ask playing into his little story.

"All I could think about was sharing another beer with you. Preferably in a hot tub again. So, I decided there was no way I was going to look handsome on this date. Nope, I didn't need some sister falling for me when I have my beer drinking sweetheart waiting for me."

"Well, I think you look mighty handsome. I can't wait to see what you look like when you get all cleaned up."

"Next!" the young kid behind the counter shouts.

"Two VIP tickets please."

"Connor, you don't have to do that. VIP is expensive."

"I don't care. It's the only way I can guarantee to get you alone." The deep, sexy tone of his voice causes a wetness to pool in my panties I haven't felt in such a long time.

"C'mon, let's go wait in line." Connor grabs my hand and pulls me along behind him.

"So, you really didn't know?"

"What?"

"That I was your date tonight?"

"I was as shocked as you. Colton told me he met some hot island girl who was just visiting for a few weeks. Never did I think my best friend's date was the same girl I've noticed picking up and dropping off Aaron at school all week."

"Yeah, she's been hanging out with little man in the afternoon so he doesn't have to go to the babysitter until I get off work."

"He looks much happier when she's there."

"Well, I'm sure he is. They are each other's only aunt and nephew. They have a very special bond. I wish she could stay longer. So, what do you do that makes you able to pick up London every day? I love her name, by the way."

"I'm a freelance sports writer. So, I make my own schedule. What do you do?"

"Real estate agent. I work for Addyson's office. The hours suck and I hate to leave Aaron for the open houses on the weekends, but it's what pays the bills. And I'm kinda good at it." I laugh.

"If you could do anything in the world, what would you do?"

"Something with special needs children. I'm not sure what, but something. In Hawaii, our neighbor's son had down syndrome and the days I babysat him were some of the best memories I took with me. I hope he's still there when we go back this summer."

"You're going to Hawaii?" he asks.

"Yeah, Aaron needs to see his grandparents."

"Evans. VIP. Party of two."

"That's us." Connor slides his hand around my waist and leads me into the Ferris wheel cart. As we sit down, I realize Connor's arm is still wrapped around me and ever so subtly pulling me closer to him. Knowing this is hurdle number one, I let my body relax into his.

"Is this ok?" I ask.

"Perfect," Connor whispers in my ear, causing goosebumps to form on every inch of my body.

"Oh, my goodness, Connor. The view is spectacular." I stand up to take in the entire view in front of me. Because of the late sunset and the lingering clouds from a storm which recently passed through, the sky is a breathtaking shade of purple. Lights from the restaurants on the pier are reflecting off the water and creating a soft glow through the bottom of the glass floor of the cart.

"Definitely the most gorgeous thing I've seen in a very long time," he says.

"The sky or the water?"

"You."

"Connor." I turn toward him and meet those amazingly perfect eyes dead on.

"You are stunning, Daniella. I know you were probably expecting some muscled-up guy when you found out you were being set up with one of Colton's friends, but if you just give me a chance—"

Before Connor can continue with any crazier thoughts, I do it. I make the first move. I slide my arms around his neck, stretch up on my tiptoes and take his lips in mine. The kiss slowly deepens as Connor pulls my body into his.

My tongue gently traces his soft lips, and as if on a mission, finds its way to Connor's. His hands glide along my back, finding their way into my hair and pulling my mouth closer to his. Never in my life have I found the taste of cigarettes and beer appealing, but tonight I find it panty-dropping sexy.

A soft moan escapes my lips as we begin to pull apart. Connor places a few pecks on my cheeks, tickling my face with his beard, before coming forehead to forehead with me.

"Damn, sweetheart," he softly says.

"What?" I ask.

"I need to be careful."

"Of what?" I feel the smile starting to escape my lips.

"Your lips may become my newest addiction," Connor says with a growl in his voice.

"I think I could live with that." He leans down and takes control. His hand grips my hair and pulls me to him. Our teeth crash, our tongues wrestle, our bodies ache, but I know we need to slow down. Damn, I've missed being touched by a man.

It's been close to two years since I've even kissed someone. Hell, the last time I had sex was before Makoa was deployed for his last tour. Oh shit. Makoa. My husband. I pull myself away from Connor and will away the tears from flooding my eyes.

"Sweetheart? Baby, what's wrong?"

"Nothing, I'm fine," I lie.

"Daniella, you are not fine. Tell me what's wrong. I told you the other night in the hot tub any guy who gets the privilege of dating you, must understand all of you."

"You're the first guy I've kissed in almost two years. Mak was deployed for almost four months before he died."

"Sweetheart, I'm sorry. If you're not ready, we can slow down. I'd love to see where this might go. I like you and you are one amazing kisser."

"Thank you," I say reaching up and kissing him again. "And I'm so glad it was you tonight. So damn glad," I repeat. I turn myself around to enjoy the view before our time is up. Connor wraps his arms around me and holds me. And for the first time in a long while, I feel safe.

"Our ride's almost over. Are you ready to go home?" he asks.

"No. Are you? Do you need to go get the girls?"

"Nope. Slumber party at the neighbors. Aaron?"

"Sleep over at Kevin's."

"He's a good kid. He was in London's preschool class. So, what do you want to do?" Connor asks.

"What's over there?" I point to what looks like a hopping night spot.

"The Crab Crawl. You wanna go have a few drinks and go dancing?"

"I don't know. Can you dance? I don't want you embarrassing me or anything," I tease.

"You just wait, sweetheart. Even for a big guy, I've got some sexy moves."

Connor grabs my hand, spins me a couple times and dips me down. When he pulls me back up, our eyes lock.

"Damn, you're beautiful." His words cause my cheeks to burn. "And you're cuter when you blush." Connor pulls me into another quick kiss before our ride comes to an end. A softer, much sweeter kiss than the previous ones. One which will cause my lady bits to tingle for the rest of the night.

CHAPTER SEVEN

THANK GOD FOR MRS. Fletcher and her sleepovers. If I had said no to Colton, he would have found someone else to go with him, and Daniella would be here with some random guy from the bar. The last thing this woman's fragile heart needs is some one-night stand screwing with it.

By the time we get to the bar, the place is already packed with the typical weekend crowd. The Crab Crawl is one of the few places in the area featuring live music and dancing, so people of all ages like to gather. A group of twenty-something women are having a bachelorette party in the corner, singles in their thirties and forties trying to find someone to go home with are scattered through the crowd, and the most hilarious older couple in their sixties are just dancing the night away with not a care in the world.

"Dance or drink?" I ask.

"Let's get a drink first," Daniella suggests.

"To the bar!" I grab her hand and pull her through the crowd behind me.

After squeezing into an empty spot, we wait for the bartender to make her way to us. Daniella's body is pushed up close to mine and my dick immediately reacts. The purple sweater she's wearing hugs her body tight and with each breath, I watch her amazing tits move up and down. And damn those jeans. They shape her ass like a perfect peach I want to sink my teeth into. She is fucking gorgeous.

"What can I get you?" the young bartender directly asks me.

"A Blue Moon and for you sweetheart?" I ask looking at my date who was obviously being ignored.

"A double shot of tequila and a Corona please."

"Tequila, huh?"

"When in Rome!" She laughs.

"What the hell does that mean?" I ask.

"I don't get out like this very often, so when I do, I want to let loose."

The bartender brings us our drinks and before Daniella's shot glass even hits the bar, she has downed her shot and asked for another. She throws back the second double shot just as fast.

"Damn, girl. Slow down."

"C'mon. Let's dance."

For the next couple hours, Daniella and I drink, dance, and kiss. A lot. The taste of tequila on her lips is intoxicating; the more I taste her, the more I want her.

"Take me home," she whispers against my lips.

"Anything you wish, sweetheart."

Outside the bar, waiting in the chilly night air for our Uber to arrive, Daniella starts to hum a familiar tune. I knew it was coming, but who am I to stop her. Right as she gets to the chorus, she belts out, "Tequila makes her clothes fall off!"

Oh shit. Daniella's much more drunk than I thought. Time to get this girl home.

"We're going to the Northern Lights community in Redmond," I instruct the driver.

"You don't live in Northern Lights. You live in Blue Dreams," Daniella slurs.

"You are correct sweetheart."

"Oh. My. Goodness." She puts her hands over her mouth like she's just discovered a secret she's not supposed to know.

"What?"

"I just realized our neighborhoods are named after—" Daniella looks around to see if anyone is listening.

"Pot strains."

The Uber driver and I both crack up laughing. "Sweetheart, how do you know that?"

"Something I saw on the news about Washington top selling strains. I retain random facts. Connor?"

"Yes?"

"I like you." She curls up next to me and starts to snore.

Daniella's snoring got progressively louder the closer we got to home. Twenty minutes in I realized I have no idea where this sleeping beauty lives.

"Shit," I mumble under my breath.

"Something wrong, man?" the driver asks.

"I just realized I don't know where my date lives."

"It's cool, man. I do," he says with a laugh.

"Excuse me?"

"I'm Jamal. Coincidently, I was Daniella and Leilani's ride to the Space Needle. I'm glad her date worked out for her."

"Why do say that?" I ask suspiciously.

"She was worried about you being some cocky gym rat like your friend." His comment made me smile. At times, having Colton as a best friend has been a blessing. Other times have been a downright fucking curse. He is the absolute greatest guy in the world; he would give you his last dime if you asked. Yet, being his dating wingman has sucked ass.

Colton is what the ladies call perfection, or so I've heard them say many times. Perfectly sculpted abs, panty-melting smile, and a southern accent which makes women swoon. Then there's me. The single dad, with the single dad bod…and maybe a few more. Once I had a woman tell me what I lack in body, I make up in personality. What the fuck?

It's why I hate dating; it's a scene I have virtually no experience in. I married young and haven't been divorced long. I raise two young girls on my own, so my ex-wife can have an awesome military career. I have no time to spend hours in the gym worrying about what I look like. For a good part of my day I'm on my ass writing just so I can put food on my kids table.

"We're here," Jamal informs me. "Do you want me to wait?"

"Please. Give me like ten minutes."

"No problem."

First, I grab the keys out of the side pocket of Daniella's purse and stuff them in my pocket. Jamal helps with the car door and I scoop her into my arms to take her inside. Blindly, I make my way through her place searching for her room. After three attempts, I finally find it.

Placing Daniella on the bed, she instantly curls up into a tiny little ball, reminding me of a hedgehog. I take her boots off and place them next to the bed. Next, I go into the bathroom and find aspirin and a glass of water and leave it on her nightstand because this girl is going to wake up with one hell of a hangover. Finally, I cover her with a blanket, kiss her on the forehead and head toward the door.

"Connor," she mumbles from the bed.

"Yeah, sweetheart?"

"Thank you."

"DADDY, I WANT TO wear my butterfly wings today," London says running into my room and jumping onto my bed.

"Cool with me. Might be easier for Harper to keep an eye on you if you're floating around in bright pink wings."

"Why do I have to watch her today? I want to hang out with my friends too," Harper comes in whining.

"Ask your sister, she's the one who volunteered me."

"Daddy gets to spend some time in the dunk tank today. People are going to throw baseballs at him for an hour. It's the kindergarten booth!"

"You've got to be kidding me, right?" The one joy I get as a father is embarrassing my twelve-year-old daughter in front of her friends.

"Hey, if you don't like it, don't go," I tell her flatly.

"Whatever, Dad," she huffs before storming out of the room.

"Lose the attitude, princess."

"It's because she wants to ride the Ferris wheel with Tanner Walker. She thinks she's going to get her first kiss on the ride."

"And how do you know this young lady?"

"Harper's loud when she's on the phone."

"Harper's never loud."

"The walls are thin."

"No, they're not. London, you need to stop spying on your sister."

"Fine. But you know I'm good intel."

"Where do you learn these things?" I ask laughing.

"Disney Channel."

"Go get dressed. We're leaving in thirty minutes."

The main reason I bought a house in Redmond is because it has some of the best schools in the state of Washington. The PTA is a perky group of middle-aged women who've been running the school for years. These women bombarded me the moment they found out I was a single dad with a flexible schedule. Can I build props for the play? Can I lift all the boxes of cans from the food drive? One even asked me to give her son the talk because her husband ran off with his secretary. No, yes, and hell no!

The carnival is being held at the local high school to accommodate the expected crowds. Apparently, this is one of the largest events of the year, being a joint effort between the elementary, middle, and high schools. I'm told it's a pretty good time.

Daniella and I haven't spoken since last weekend. We've sent a few texts back and forth, but both our schedules have been insane and we keep missing each other. I did, however, suggest we meet for ice cream this afternoon. I mean, the least I can do is make London treat Aaron to an ice cream after treating him so poorly.

"So how long do I have to watch her?" Harper whines as we are getting out of my truck.

"I don't know. How bad do you want to ride the Ferris wheel with Tanner Walker?"

"How do you…" she stammers.

"'Cause I'm yo' daddy, baby girl. I know everything. Harper, if you want more responsibility as a babysitter, then you need to work for it."

"Wait. Is this a babysitting *job*?" She makes sure to put extra emphasis on the word job.

"If you don't lose her, then yes. Eight bucks an hour is what I'll pay you."

"Deal." Might as well make her earn the money I was going to give her anyways.

Walking up to the seven-foot dunk tank, I'm kicking myself in the ass for getting myself into this. The excitement I see in London's little chubby cheeks, makes getting dunked worth it.

"Ms. Johnston said she was happy you volunteered because not many parents did," London says.

"You know I love to help, munchkin. Alright, Harper you're on duty. Come back here in about an hour and you can go on your date."

"It's not a date," she huffs.

"Can I try and dunk you, Daddy?"

"Sure! Here's twenty bucks for each of you. Be good." Both my girls run off hand in hand to exchange their money for tickets.

"Thank you so much for helping us out today, Mr. Evans," Ms. Johnston comes up from behind and startles me. She puts her hand on my arm before she continues. "You know we don't get many dads who volunteer like you do."

"I'm glad to help. Are we ready to get started?" I ask.

"Of course. Climb up the ladder in the back and into the cage," she instructs.

Sitting on the bench, I dangle my feet down and into the frigid water below. Today is unusually warm for mid-March in Washington, but I'll take it. Ms. Johnston gets on her bullhorn announcing the tank is now open for dunking. Before she even finishes her sentence, the line is already fifteen people deep.

Out of the corner of my eye, I see a curly-haired little boy grab on the leg of his teacher. "Ms. Johnston! Ms. Johnston!" he shouts.

"Hey Aaron! You and your mom having fun?"

"Yes! I want to eat cotton candy. Blue is my favorite."

"Well, you better head over to the third-grade booth before it's all gone," she says.

"Aaron, leave Ms. Johnston alone. She has to make sure Mr. Evans gets dunked, buddy," Daniella says with a cute little smirk.

"Mommy! I want to try!"

"Sure. Why not? Six balls, Ms. Johnston."

"Here you go," she says.

Aaron steps up to the line and raises his arm to throw the ball. When he releases it, the ball hits the ground and rolls just two feet away. He tries a couple more times and the results are exactly the same.

He hands the last two balls to his mother. "You do it. I stink." The disappointment in his eyes hits me. I've seen it before many times in my daughters. Whenever they need something girly, like a braid. Braids are the damn worst.

Daniella attempts to throw the last two balls and her throws are just as sad as Aaron's.

"Oh well," Aaron says deflated. "I really wanted the first dunk."

"Little man, come here," I shout. He turns around and sprints to the front of the tank.

"Yeah?" he asks.

"Would you like to come play baseball in the park tomorrow afternoon with me and London?"

"Can I Mom? Can I?" He jumps up and down with excitement.

"I think we can make that happen," Daniella says. Moments like these are just as hard for her as they are for her son. I want to be the person who helps make her strong again.

"Aaron," I whisper.

"Yeah," he attempts to whisper back but is way too loud.

"Go hit the bullseye. I'm hot and need to cool off."

"Isn't that cheating?" he asks innocently.

"Not if I told you to," I explain.

Aaron runs to the bullseye and pushes the target with both hands as hard as he can. After a couple failed attempts, he pushes up his shirt sleeves, growls, and pushes as hard as his little body will allow. His last push is all it takes for me to drop into the tank below. I'm a big guy and with that comes a big splash. Anyone within a few feet of the dunk tank felt the effects of my drop.

"Awesome, Daddy!" I hear London scream as I emerge from the freezing water.

"I'm glad I could entertain you, munchkin."

"Good job, Aaron!" I see her raise her hand and the two friends clumsily miss their high five. Wow, aren't these two a pair?

"Wanna go get cotton candy with me?" he asks.

"Can I go?" London asks her sister.

"Sure. See you in forty-five minutes, Dad."

"Awesome! I'll be here. Getting wet. By myself." I wave them off wishing I was with them instead of in a damn dunking tank.

"I'll keep you company," Ms. Johnston says, batting her eyelashes at me. Holy shit. Is my daughter's teacher trying to flirt with me?

"Thanks," I grumble.

The next hour flies by quickly and I only end up getting dunked a few times. A handful of the dads of students here at Burdi Elementary play for a local minor league baseball team. Last season, I wrote a harsh article about how poorly they were playing; hence, only being dunked three times by them. Apparently, this was their attempt at revenge.

After using the gym locker room to dry off and put on some fresh clothes, I set out to find my girls. On my way to the dunk tank, I hear London's contagious giggle coming from the jumpy house. Standing there, watching the kids from the sides, is Daniella. Every time I see this woman, my heart skips a beat. I feel like a fucking teenager with his first crush.

"Hey." I come up from behind her and gently grab her waist. She practically jumps out of her skin.

"Connor! You startled me."

"I'm sorry. I see London and Aaron are jumping. Where's Harper?"

"Ladies room. I told her I'd watch London for her. She's been very responsible today," Daniella says.

"It's because she wants to get paid for babysitting."

112

"No, it's because you've raised a good girl, Connor. I'd love to have her watch Aaron sometime."

"Really, Ms. Kahele?" Harper asks, joining the conversation.

"Yes, sweetheart. You did an excellent job with both kids today. I was impressed."

"Thanks. Dad, can I go now? Bryce just texted me and is waiting at the Ferris wheel."

"Sure. Check back in an hour." She reaches up and kisses my cheek before running off to meet some boy.

"Wanna go ride the Ferris wheel?" I ask.

"No. We are not going to spy on your daughter's first kiss."

"How do you know he's going to kiss her?" I ask.

"We talked a bit as the kids were playing. I think she just needed to open up to someone."

"She knows she can talk to me."

"Yeah, but you're her dad. Definitely not the person she wants to talk to about boys."

"Thank you."

"Of course. Maybe you can repay me by helping little man learn to throw a ball."

"Now there's something I'm good at." I laugh.

The four of us spend the rest of the afternoon eating as much junk food as we can fit into our mouths, playing games and enjoying a picturesque day outside. The first time we run into Harper and Tanner, she pretends not to know us. The second time she ignores us, I send London in to do her annoying little sister routine. And of course, Aaron wants to join in. Pure comedy. Yet, when she does it a third time, she needs to be taught a lesson. Embarrassing dad mode initiated.

Just as I'm about pull my pants up Urkel high, Daniella puts her hand on my arm to stop me. "Don't do that to her, Connor,"

"Isn't it my job as a dad to embarrass her?" I tease.

"You really want to humiliate your daughter in front of the first boy she's ever really liked? There will be plenty of other situations you can embarrass her, but don't do it on her first date."

"Harper's only twelve. She's too young to be dating."

"But she's not too young to like a boy and hang out with her friends. Look at her over there. You can see Harper's got herself into a good group of kids. You're doing a fantastic job with her."

"Thanks. Now, speaking of first dates, when are we going to go on ours?" I ask.

"Sorry. No can do. Kinda already dating someone," she says.

"You are?"

"Yep. We went out last weekend, had this toe-curling first kiss overlooking the city, he let me drink all my cares away, and then tucked me into bed. I'm not sure if you could top a first date like his." Her deep chocolate eyes get this amazing twinkle as she talks about our first kiss.

"That was not a first date. We were set up and it happened to be with each other. I would like to take you out on a proper first date."

"I think I'd rather have a second date with the man who's already sweeping me off my feet."

"I will see if he's available." Lost in the moment, I lean in to kiss those luscious, soft lips.

"Mommy!" Aaron shouts.

"Daddy!" London screams.

As if broken from a trance, Daniella and I quickly jump three feet apart from each other. Kids and dating can be a tricky situation.

"What's next? What's next?" Both kids are shouting in unison.

"What would you like to do, munchkin?"

"Ride the Ferris wheel!" London exclaims.

"I'm sorry, baby. Daddy was told to stay away from the Ferris wheel.

"I'll take her," Daniella volunteers.

"Well, Aaron, the high school's JROTC cadets are about to put on a demonstration. Would you like to go watch it with me?" I ask.

"What's JROTC?" he asks, messing it all up.

"Those are the students who want to join the military after they graduate."

"Like my daddy?"

"Just like your daddy," I explain.

"Mommy, can I go?" he asks Daniella.

"Of course."

Aaron puts his little hand in mine, and practically bouncing, we take off in the other direction.

When I look back at Daniella and London waiting in line. The smiles across both their faces are happy and for the first time since Eva left, I'm starting to feel something again.

Teri Kay

CHAPTER EIGHT

Daniella

T HIS PAST WEEKEND REMINDED me of something in one of those cheesy romantic comedies with Tom Hanks or Matthew McConaughey I love so much. Sunday afternoon, we met Connor and his daughters at the park for lunch and baseball.

Watching Connor teach my son how to throw a ball caused a wrestling match in my heart. On one hand, I am so grateful Connor has come into our lives and is willing to spend time with Aaron, but it also makes me realize how much I miss Makoa.

"Everything ok?" Leilani asks, entering my room.

"Yeah, just thinking about my weekend with Connor. And Mak."

"Makoa would want to see you happy, Dani. Now, speaking of happy," she says.

"Yes?" I question with a suspicious brow.

"I love Seattle."

"Seattle or Colton?"

"Seattle. But Colton doesn't hurt. I'd like to stay. Like, maybe permanently," Leilani says.

"If your parents say it's ok, then you can stay here."

"I'm twenty-five. I don't need to ask my parents if I can move away from Hawaii."

I throw my hands on my hips in a motherly way. "Really?"

"Right!" She laughs. "I already did. Papa said it's fine as long as I'm living with you and not some howli."

"Does he forget your mother and I are howlis?"

"Sometimes I think he does."

Later that evening, just as I'm about to close my eyes, my text message alerts three times in a row.

Connor- Hi Daniella

Connor- You still awake?

Connor- Can I ask you something?

Connor seems so confident in person, and yet I sense some nervousness in his text messages.

Me- I am. And you may.

Unexpectedly, my phone starts to ring instead of sending me a text message alert. What the hell?

"Hello?"

"Hi Daniella. How are you?"

"I'm fine," I say with a slight giggle alerting him to my confusion.

"What are you laughing about?"

"The nineties called. They want their telephone call back."

"You are such a smartass," he teases.

"Dude, seriously? Who calls anymore?"

"Me. It's more personal."

Without thinking, I hang up on Connor. Last weekend at the carnival I noticed we have the same phone. "Here goes nothing," I whisper to myself.

I hit the video chat button and call Connor back. He answers after one ring.

"This is personal," I tell him.

"It is. I love it. I wasn't sure if you liked video chatting or not."

"I do. You said you wanted something more personal. For me it's either text or video chat. In my life, phone calls have only brought sad news. I don't want any more unwelcome news in my life."

"Do you think someone asking you out on a date would be considered unwelcome news?" he asks.

"I don't know. Depends," I sass.

"On?"

"Who that someone is."

"Me. Who else would it be? It's me, smartass." He laughs. When Connor laughs, he smiles. When he smiles, I get goosebumps.

Leilani peeks her head in when she hears me talking and I wave her into bed with me.

"I don't know. Guys ask girls out all the time for their friends. How do I know you're not asking me out for Colton?"

"Because that fiery little five-foot sister of yours would kick both our asses."

"Yes, I would! Hawaiian girls don't mess around," Leilani says yanking the phone into her view. "Now, Mr. Connor Karaoke, I believe you had something to ask me."

"Yes, I did, Ms. Feisty Blonde. Would you like to go out with me Saturday?"

"I don't know if I can. Leilani's going home for a couple weeks to pack her things to move to Seattle to help Aaron and I out."

"I think Harper can handle the two munchkins for a couple hours during the afternoon," Connor explains.

"Then it's a date. See you Saturday, Mr. Karaoke."

"See you then, sweetheart." With a click I end the video chat.

"Did he just call you sweetheart?" Leilani asks.

"He did. He called me sweetheart a few times the other night. I think for him it's just a casual thing."

"I don't know, Dani. He sounded serious to me. I think Connor really likes you."

"I like him, also. I'm just worried we are in two completely separate places. He's been dating. I'm just starting again."

"Well, whatever happens, remember the Gods will always send you somebody to love," Leilani says.

"What?" I question.

"I don't know; it's just something silly my brother used to say to me. Always stuck with me. Alright, time for bed. Good night, sister. Love you."

"I love you, too, Leilani. I'm glad you're staying."

Drifting off to sleep, I know my night will be filled with thoughts and dreams of Makoa. Or maybe Connor.

"He looks just like you," I tell my husband as we watch our son splash on the beach of Wai'anapanaa in Maui on our annual camping trip.

"I have good genes. What can I say?" He laughs.

"Yes, you do. I can only hope he grows up as handsome as you."

"And as smart as you," Makoa says.

"We are one lucky family." I lean back, and he wraps his strong arms around me.

"You're going to do a fantastic job with him. Don't be afraid to let him play football or climb trees. And you better teach him how to surf."

"Mak, what are you talking about? You'll teach him all those things."

"Dani, I want you to be happy. You're smile brightens up any room and so many people need that in their life. Let him make you happy."

"No more Mai Tais for you, young man," I tease.

"I gotta go, baby. You and little man are going to be just fine."

Before I can say anything else, Makoa is at the shoreline kissing Aaron on the head, and then dives into the next wave. I scream his name and go running after him, but he's gone.

I'm jolted out of bed when Leilani comes rushing in my room. "Are you ok? You were yelling Mak's name."

"Yeah. Just a dream. I'm fine. Thanks for checking."

"Girl, your soaking wet. That must have been some dream."

"Beaches of Maui. What can I say? I'm fine though, really. Can you just grab me a bottle of water please?"

"What the hell was that all about?" I mumble, throwing myself back against the pillows.

THIS WEEK HAS LITERALLY been a shit storm. Leilani left for Hawaii on Tuesday and because of a random chicken truck accident on the freeway, she barely made her flight. Aaron's been upset about having to go back to the babysitter causing him to act out, both at home and at school. Damn kid kicked a fourth grader in the breakfast line because the kid took the last chocolate milk. Not to mention, I also had two houses fall out of escrow.

My date with Connor is the only thing keeping me going this week. It has been my light at the end of the tunnel. We agreed on an afternoon date, since Harper is still new to babysitting and she's never babysat two kids at once.

"Hey Momma!" Aaron says running into my room and bouncing on my bed. "You look pretty. I like your shirt. Where are we going?"

"Would you like to go hang out with London for a little while?" I ask.

"I'd rather hang out with Kevin."

"Well, I thought you could hang out with London and her sister for a few hours this afternoon."

"You'll be there, right?"

"No, honey, I won't be."

"Will Mr. Connor?"

"No baby. Mr. Connor and I are going to go have lunch."

"So, no adults?" Aaron asks, worry fills his eyes.

"Harper will be watching you and London," I explain. "Are you ok with that?"

"I… I guess," his voice hitches and shoulders sag.

I can't do this. Aaron feeling secure is more important than a date. Hopefully, Connor understands.

"Hello?" Connor answers. Even just answering the phone his voice is buttery.

"Hi Connor. I have some bad news."

"What's up, sweetheart?"

"Aaron is nervous about being alone without an adult. He's never been left alone before."

"You still want to spend the afternoon together?" he asks.

"I've been looking forward to it all week," I say, obviously disappointed.

"I'll be there in thirty minutes to pick you guys up. Do you have a booster for Aaron or do you want me to grab my extra?"

Oh my god. Did this guy really just ask about a booster seat for my son? "An extra would be great."

"See you soon, gorgeous."

Exactly thirty minutes later, I hear London bouncing up the walkway. "C'mon Dad. Hurry up! Let's go get Aaron and his mom and tell them our surprise."

Her little hand creates the softest knock on my door and excitement for the day replaces my nervousness.

"Hi London."

"Hi, Ms. Daniella. Is Aaron ready? Can I go get him?"

"Sure sweetie. He's in his room at the top of the stairs." She's up the stairs before I can even finish my sentence.

"Hey," I say turning my attention to Connor. "I'm so sorry our date got ruined."

"Who said anything about it being ruined? Just changed a little. Daniella, we both have kids. Plans are going to change all the time. Just one of the downfalls to dating with young children. I want Aaron to feel comfortable. I don't care what we do as long as I get to spend some time with you."

Connor looks over his shoulder to see if Harper is watching us and then over my shoulder to check for the younger two. When he realizes the coast is clear, he gently places his lips on mine and kisses me. "I've been dying to taste these lips since last week."

"I really wanted some alone time with you," I whisper.

"We'll get it. I promise."

"We're ready!" Aaron and London shout as they come bounding down the stairs.

"Alright, let's head out to the car," I instruct.

Just as excited as the kids, I bounce down the walkway and hop into Connor's fully loaded GMC Denali.

"Did you tell Aaron where we were going?" Connor asks.

"Nope! Did you tell Ms. Dani?"

"Sure didn't."

"Awesome! I love surprises!" London shouts.

"But you can't keep a secret for longer than five minutes to save your life," Harper chimes in from the back seat of the large SUV.

"Yes, I can," London argues.

"No, she can't," Connor agrees.

"Where are we going?" I ask.

"You'll see." He laughs.

When Connor smiles at me, I feel safe, like it's ok to laugh out loud again. All I really want is a best friend to grow old with. Someone who will hold me through scary movies. Someone who will laugh at our children with me. Someone who will love and protect my bruised and broken heart.

At the stop light, we both instinctively turn back and check on the kids, who all seem to be totally engrossed in Trolls. I don't think Aaron has ever been in a car with a television before. We take the few brief seconds to steal some private glances before the light turns green.

"Hey kids. Daniella and I were thinking about putting in a karaoke CD. Wanna sing with us?"

"No, Dad, please," London whines.

"Haven't you figured it out yet? Whenever Dad says he wants to sing karaoke in the car, it means he wants us to put on the headphones," Harper explains.

"Oh. Well, why doesn't he just say that?" her little sister asks.

"'Cause he's a boy and boys are confusing. Now here," she hands them both earphones. "Put these on."

"Thanks, sweet pea."

"She's a good kid, Connor. You are doing an amazing job with them," I say, when all the kids are no longer able to hear us.

"Thanks. It's getting easier as they are getting older and we're figuring it out along the way. How are you and Aaron adjusting to life in Seattle?"

"I mean, it's the same for us. We're figuring it out day by day. Raising a little man is a challenge. Especially since he has his father's overwhelming sense of stubbornness. Damn that kid can be hard-headed at times."

"Yeah, try raising a twelve-year-old girl. Puberty is overwhelming," he sighs.

"I remember being a preteen girl. You win," I tease.

"I used to have Nicolette to help me out with anything girly, but we haven't talked since the wedding. I've tried a couple times and it always goes to voicemail."

"I can ask Addyson if you want. I know she's close to her cousin, Brad."

"Nope. If Nic doesn't want to talk to me, then that's on her."

I need to change the subject before Connor's grip on the steering wheel gets any tighter.

"So, where are we going?"

"The zoo. Sound good?"

"You are going to become Aaron's new favorite person. First the JROTC performance, which he can't stop talking about by the way, and now the zoo. Please tell me they have penguins."

"Yeah they do. Why?"

"Penguins are Aaron's favorite animal and they never had any at the Oahu Zoo. He is going to freak out. Thank you for doing this for us Connor." I want so badly to reach over and grab his hand, but I'm not sure how Aaron will react if he sees me holding another man's hand. Is holding hands something Connor would even do in front of his girls? He was right. Dating with kids is a bitch.

During the forty-five-minute drive to the zoo, we make small talk and start to get to know each other better, just like you would on any first date. We agree to keep the day easy and fun, no talk to bring down the mood of our day.

In our conversation, I learn he's a huge sports fan, but it was his love of baseball which lead him to be a sports writer. Connor's favorite food is a real California burrito, potato fries and all, but he'll do anything for a Ding-Dong. And he loves real country music, not this pop country that's out now, like Luke Bryan. I told him it might be the deal breaker in this relationship. He laughed; I was dead serious.

"Where are we, Mommy?" Aaron shouts forgetting he has on the headphones.

"Read the sign. You can read now."

"Z-o-o," he sounds out. "Zoo. Are we really at the zoo?"

"Yes, we are little man."

"See, I kept it a secret," London proclaims.

"That's just 'cause the Trolls made you forget," Harper chimes in.

Piling out of the SUV, I watch Aaron approach Connor and say something to him, but he talks so soft and the girls are chattering behind me, I can't hear what it is. They do the most adorable little high-five and then Aaron turns and runs to my side.

"Mommy! Mommy! They have real penguins!"

"Well, we're just going to have to go see those aren't we? Did you thank Mr. Connor?"

"Thank you, Mr. Connor."

"Of course, buddy! Let's go see those penguins now." Connor puts out both his hands and Aaron and London each run up and grab a finger. I try to fight back the tears welling up in my eyes. I've often wondered how Aaron would react if another man came into our lives but seeing the ear-to-ear smile on his face makes me think he'll be ok. But the question remains, will I?

"Alright Harper. You ready for this?" Connor asks.

"I got this dad. You two are going to be impressed with my skills." Harper grabs a map of the zoo and the younger kids and begins to map out where they want to go today.

"What's going on?" I question.

"I told Harper today was her babysitting test to see if she can handle two kids at once. That way she can watch them, Aaron feels safe and we can still get some alone time," he explains.

"Did it hurt?" I ask tilting my head in curiosity.

"Did what hurt?" I paused for a minute, waiting for him to take a drink of his Mountain Dew.

"When you fell from heaven, because you really are an angel." And there it is. The laugh, the choke and out the nose. This causes me to laugh so hard my sides begin to hurt. The kids are staring at us like we are two of the craziest people in the world.

"Are you guys done being weird? We're ready to go see aminals!" London shouts.

"It's animals, munchkin," Connor corrects her.

"That's what I said, aminals."

Because of Aaron's excitement for the penguin exhibit, we decide to head there first. I will admit, I'm just as eager to see the exhibit, since I've never seen a penguin in real life either. The first time I ever went to a zoo was when Makoa took me in Honolulu at the age of twenty-five.

Aaron and London are a bit overly excited as we go through the indoor penguin enclosure. Each time one of the little birds jumps into the water, these two squeal like it's the best thing they've ever seen. Harper unsuccessfully works on keeping them quiet while we stand in the back and giggle. Their excitement is contagious as the people around them start to laugh and squeal each time a penguin dives in.

Reaching the end of the exhibit, we come to the Arctic simulator ride. I've never been fond of these types of rides. Being jerked around in front of a movie screen full of snow is not on my list of fun things to do today. Hopefully, this is one of those moments where Connor planned some alone time.

"Who wants to go on the Arctic ride with me?" Harper asks.

"Mommy hates these kinds of rides. She threw up on the Star Wars ride one time in front of her boyfriend before she met my daddy."

"You remember too much kid," I groan.

"How about I take the kids on the ride and you guys go get us some lunch over there." She points to a pizza place.

"Sounds like a good plan to me. Here," Connor hands her some money, "stop at the penguin gift shop on your way out." Before I can even get my hand in my purse to give Aaron some money, the kids are running down the hall to the ride entrance.

"Crap. Aaron walked off before I could give him any money."

"Stop it, Daniella. I handed her enough money for all three of them. This is my date. My treat."

Glancing around, I try to find a secluded spot to pull Connor off to. Somewhere not surrounded by kids. I spot a grassy, picnic table area with a large tree right in the middle which is empty.

I grab Connor's hand and pull him behind me like two silly teenagers. Needing to take control of the moment, I push his back against the tree, stand on the tips of my toes and press my lips to his. I place my arms around his neck and pull my body closer to him. Deepening the kiss, my tongue starts to explore his mouth. Connor's hands move down my back and take a firm grip on my ass. A moan much louder than I intended escaped my lips.

"I love your ass," he whispers in my ear causing goosebumps to cover my body.

I feel his phone ringing in his pocket. "Is that your phone vibrating or you just happy to see me?" I laugh.

"Shit. It's Harper and we haven't even gotten the pizza yet. Hey, Harper. Everything ok?" he answers, putting her on speaker phone.

"Hey Dad. Yeah, the kids are fine. So, I guess there's a new lovebird show here at the zoo."

"Ok, cool. We'll go see it later," he suggests.

"Oh, I've already seen it. Right through the window of the gift shop." I look up and see Harper smiling and waving her fingers at her father and me. Shit.

"Harper Leigh, go pay for London and Aaron's stuff and stop spying on me." Connor hangs up on his daughter.

"Busted," I sheepishly say.

"So, fucking worth it." Connor throws his arms around me, taking a firm grip on my ass and takes control of my mouth one more time before the kids return from their shopping spree.

CHAPTER
NINE

"DADDY, DADDY," LONDON'S LITTLE fingers are poking me in the side. "Wake up, Daddy."

"What? What's wrong?" I ask, still half asleep.

"I don't know. Harper is crying in the bathroom. I tried to ask her what was wrong but she yelled at me to go away."

"You go downstairs and watch cartoons. I'll deal with your sister."

I drag myself out of bed and throw on the gray sweatpants I left laying on the floor. I slept like shit last night and I'm not in the mood for Harper's preteen drama.

"Harper? What's going on? You need to come out of the bathroom so London can get ready for school."

"No! I'm not coming out! I'm not going to school!" she screams.

"Harper Leigh," I say firmly. "What is going on?"

"You're a guy. You wouldn't understand."

Oh shit. I know exactly what's going on. "Honey, I was married to your mom long enough to understand girl things. Did you start your period?"

"Oh my god, Dad! Leave me alone." I can hear her crying through the bathroom door and know there is nothing I can do to make her feel better in this situation. Nicolette still isn't answering my calls, my mom is on a cruise, Eva is on assignment, and I have no desire to ask my ex-mother-in-law for help.

"Hello?" she answers, obviously confused on why I'm calling at seven-thirty on a Tuesday morning.

"Hey Daniella. It's Connor."

"Yeah, I see you've programmed my phone as Stud Muffin Connor." Her giggle makes me smile, even in my moment of crisis. "What can I do for you this early Tuesday morning?"

"I have no idea what to do. Harper started her," I pause, taking a deep breath, "first period and there is not a female around to help her with this. I have everything here for her, but I have no idea how to use any of these sticky pads and tampon do-hickeys."

"Oh my goodness Connor! Don't ever call them do-hickeys again. Give her the instructions to read over and tell her I'll be there in five minutes."

It is less than five minutes later and she is already at my door. "Damn, you're fast."

"We were already in the car ready to head to the babysitter," she explains. "Where's Harper?"

"Upstairs, first door on your left. You had breakfast yet, little man?"

"Nope. I usually eat this creamy wheaty stuff at the babysitter's house," Aaron informs me.

"Well, not today. Would you like some blueberry pancakes?" I ask.

"Yes, please"

"Me too, please," Daniella chimes in from the stairs while looking at me with a smile that could bring any man to his knees.

It takes fifteen minutes for Daniella to convince Harper to leave the bathroom, happily too, I may add.

"Everything good?" I ask.

"Yes. Thanks for calling Daniella," Harper says wrapping her small arms around me.

"These pancakes are delicious," my beautiful savior standing next to me says, stealing food off my plate. "Hey, can you take Aaron to school? I have to get to an open house I'm having today."

"No problem. Where's the house you're selling?"

"It's a quaint little place up on Cottage Lake," she says.

"I've got everything handled here. You go sell houses." Fuck, I want to kiss her so damn bad. I want to tell her have a wonderful day and I'll see her tonight. Instead, I tell her to go sell houses. Fuck me.

I drop Harper off at school first and then walk the two kindergarteners to their classroom, trying to avoid Ms. Johnston, something I've been attempting to do since the uncomfortable flirting at the carnival. Just as I am about to make my escape, her call stops me in my tracks.

"Mr. Evans! Mr. Evans!"

"Hi Ms. Johnston. What can I do for you this morning?"

"In a few weeks, we will be having the annual spring barbeque, and since Mr. W retired last year, we are looking for a new grill master. I bet you are a pro on the grill. I could be your grill assistant." Did my daughter's teacher just bat her eyelashes at me?

"Sure, Ms. Johnston. Whatever you need." I tell her anything she wants to hear to escape this awkward situation.

Grabbing my usual coffee and bagel from the locally owned shop, I settle into a corner booth to finish my weekly sports column for the Washington Gazette. With the new baseball season starting up in just a few weeks, I've been asked to write my predictions and expectations for the Bremerton Brawlers upcoming season. Judging from the players dunk tank performances, I'm not expecting too much. Again.

After twenty minutes, I realize all I've managed to do is stare at the screen. Each attempt to think about baseball leads me to thinking about Daniella. When I think about catching, I think about gloves and how her ass fit in my hand like a glove. I try to think about the players running the bases and I think about the amazing kiss we shared with my hands all over her. Which base is ass-grabbing now? Is it even a base? Even the team's new colors of purple and black make me think of the outfit she wore on our first date.

"Fuck it," I whisper to myself under my breath.

The drive from Redmond to Cottage Lake usually takes twenty minutes; today I did it in twelve. I need to have my hands on her ass again. I want to run my fingers through thick, gold locks. I must claim her lips once more.

Pulling up to the address I got from her real estate agencies social media page, a red sedan pulls off leaving only Daniella's Mini Cooper in the driveway. "Here goes nothing," I whisper.

The front door is closed and I'm not sure if I should walk in or knock first. Since I don't want to scare the shit out of her, I opt to knock.

"Connor? What are you—"

Before she can finish her sentence, my hands cup her face and I bring my lips to hers. Guiding her into the house, I slam the door shut with my foot, never breaking our connection. I sweep her hair off her face, exposing a stunning neckline I've been eager to nibble on.

I move my kisses from her lips, along her cheek, and down her irresistible neck. A sexy purr escapes from her breath. Carefully, I untuck her blouse from the skirt shaping her ass into two perfect globes. My fingers run up and down her back and I feel the goosebumps form on her soft, supple skin.

"Connor," Daniella whispers. I fucking love the way she says my name.

"Yeah, sweetheart?"

"I want you so fucking bad."

"I want you to, Daniella."

She grabs my hand and leads me to one of the upstairs bedrooms. Without saying anything, this stunning woman faces me and starts unbuttoning her blouse, teasing me, one button at a time. Shimmying her shoulders, Daniella's shirt falls to the floor, but her hands immediately cover her stomach.

"Daniella, stop." I grab her hands and link them in mine as they fall at our sides. "You are gorgeous. Every single inch of you. Your luscious lips." I kiss her lips. "Your beautiful neck." I bite down her neck. "And your irresistible body." I run my finger from her collar bone to belly button.

Our mouths crash together hard, tongues greedily fighting for control. Daniella wins when she pulls my tongue from my mouth and sucks hard. My dick springs into action and is straining hard against my jeans, to the point it hurts.

My hands explore every inch of exposed skin. When I slide my fingers under the straps of her bra, Daniella moans into my mouth, letting me know she's just as turned on as I am. Using just one hand, I reach back and unsnap her bra. Running my fingers down her shoulders, I slide her bra down her arms and free her amazing tits.

"Damn, you are stunning," I say. Her nipples pebble as I run the pad of my thumb across them. Daniella's tits are a perfect size, fitting perfectly in my hand.

"This feels so good," she moans.

I sit down on the edge of the bed and pull Daniella's body close to mine. I can feel her body quiver.

"What's wrong sweetheart?"

"I haven't had sex with anyone since my husband," she quietly says.

"As much as I want to make love to you, Daniella, our first time together will not be a quickie at an open house you're hosting," I reassure her. "And contrary to the stereotype, I don't just carry condoms around in my wallet."

"Oh," she says deflated.

"Sweetheart, what's wrong?"

"Nothing."

"Baby, don't lie to me. Tell me what you want," I demand.

"I want to cum so bad, Connor."

Without another word, my hand slides up her skirt allowing my fingers to skim the edge of her panties. "You're already so wet," I growl.

"Connor," Daniella begs. "Don't tease me."

"If it makes you say my name like that, I am going to tease you again and again."

She leans down and presses her lips against mine. "I need to cum. Now."

"That's my girl." I move her panties to the side and allow her wetness to coat my fingers. Slowly, I push one finger in her eager pussy and slide my finger in and out. Her hands take a tight grip on my shoulder.

"Holy shit!"

"You like that?"

"Fuck yes," Daniella moans.

I slide a second finger in her pussy knowing she's already on the verge of cumming. Her nails dig into my shoulders, her knees begin to shake. "Connor, I'm going to cum."

I place kisses all over her exquisite tits. "Cum for me, Daniella."

"Fuck!" she screams as her body trembles against mine.

"That was beautiful, sweetheart."

"What about you?" she asks.

"Hello? Is anyone here?" a male's voice interrupts us.

"Oh shit," she says.

"I'll be right there," Daniella yells to the stranger.

"Get dressed and I'll stall for you."

"Thank you."

I lean down and kiss her once more. "I'm going to pick up Aaron today. Come have dinner with us."

"I would love to. Now go before we get caught," she teases.

Before exiting the room, I adjust my dick to try and not make my raging hard-on so fucking obvious. I find the guy wandering in the kitchen. "Hey man. Daniella will be right with you."

"Thanks." He turns around and I immediately recognize him.

"Brock Hardy."

"Connor Evans."

"You two know each other?" Daniella asks, joining us in the kitchen.

"Connor writes nasty articles in the newspaper about the team I play for, the Bremerton Brawlers."

"If you guys could play some decent ball, I would write a decent article," I quip back.

"Daniella, can you please show me the house?" he asks completely dismissing me.

"Of course. Connor, I will see you later. Thank you very much for your help with the plugged drain."

A few hours later, London, Aaron and I are wandering through the store trying to find a special dinner to make tonight. Going to the grocery store with one kindergarten child is difficult, doing it with two is nearly impossible. We quickly decide on tacos, because what goes better on a Tuesday than tacos.

The kids spend the afternoon building a fort out of old moving boxes in the backyard. By the time they finish, they've constructed a three-room box mansion fort. I'm exhausted just from watching them. I would love to have half the energy of those kids.

It is after five thirty when Daniella arrives at my house from work and she looks exhausted.

"Hey sweetheart." Greeting her at the door, I pull Daniella's body to mine and take control of her luscious lips.

"Connor!" She quickly jumps back breaking our connection. "What about the kids?"

"They're watching a movie in the mansion in the backyard."

"Mansion?"

"Don't question it. We're alone," I growl. I wrap my hands around her neck and pull Daniella's mouth back to mine. My tongue slowly explores hers, and I feel the tension of the day escape her shoulders.

"What smells so delicious?"

"Tacos. You hungry?"

"Starving. It has been a long day," she grumbles.

"Brock Hardy giving you a tough time?" I sarcastically ask, pouring us both margaritas.

"What is the beef between you two?"

"I'm honest in my writing and I don't get caught up in his smooth as butter bullshit everyone else seems to fall for. Just because you're a nice guy, whom all the women love, doesn't mean you're any good at playing baseball."

"He seems like a nice enough guy."

"Did he like the Cottage Lake house?" I inquire.

"No. He said he didn't want a house that has plugged up drains." She laughs.

"Awesome. Now he can find another realtor to buy a house from."

"Well, not exactly. He asked me to be his realtor and to help him find the perfect house in the area."

"Mommy!" Aaron greets me running in through the patio door. "I'm having so much fun with London and Mr. Connor. I learned if you blow real hard at a red light, it will turn green."

"It does, huh?" she asks.

"That's what Mr. Connor and London said, but it only worked sometimes. I think Mr. Connor does it to keep us quiet."

"You're too smart for your own good, little man," I say ruffling his brown curls. "What are you and London doing in the backyard mansion?"

"Playing with Legos. Is it almost dinner? I'm starving," he whines.

"It is. Go tell London it's time for dinner," I say.
He runs out to the patio and screams. "London! Dinner!" Then he turns around and races to be the first to the bathroom.
"Aaron!" Daniella yells at him. "I think Mr. Connor wanted you to walk to the fort—"
"Mansion, Mom. It's a mansion."

"Sorry. Mansion. Go out to the mansion and get London for dinner. Don't scream this time."

"Yes, Momma."

"I need to learn some tricks from you. I can't get London to listen to me for anything lately."

"I've got all kinds of tricks up my sleeve, handsome."
Daniella leans up and gives me one last kiss before the kids come back in for dinner.

"Guess what! Guess what! Guess what!" Harper screams busting through the front door.

"What, what, what? You hid an elephant in the backyard? You figured out time travel? Harry Styles is taking you to prom?" I tease.

"Very funny, Dad. Mom will be home for spring break and wants to take us somewhere."

"Remember Harper, your mom's schedule is always changing. Plans are always flexible with her."

"Nope, not this time. She's already got clearance and will be home in two weeks. She wants London and I to pick out where to go."

"I want to go to Las Vegas," London proclaims, bursting through the back door.

"And why is that young lady?"

"Because the town is so glittery and sparkly. I'd fit right in!"

"You're too much. Go wash up for dinner. All of you."

EVEY SINCE THE GIRLS received the phone call from their mother about the spring break trip, they have been bouncing off the walls. London even created a paper chain, counting down the days until her mom came home. Harper informed her marking the calendar was much easier, but London said she needed more visuals. God help me with this one.

"Three days, Daddy," my youngest mumbles with a mouth full of cereal. "Mommy and Heather will be here!"

"Eww, gross," her sister groans.

"I agree. Don't chew with your mouth open. I'm happy mom gets to come home and spend some time with you girls. And I'm really glad your mom agreed Las Vegas was not the best place to spend your spring break."

"Orlando is going to be so much fun," London adds.

"Mom's letting us each pick a theme park we want to do for a day."

"What did you pick?" I ask.

"Universal, Dad. Harry Potter world, duh."

"Princesses all the way for me!"

"We know," Harper and I groan in unison.

"Go get ready for school. We leave in twenty."

While doing the dishes, I hear my text message alert. Hoping it's Daniella, I'm disappointed when it's Colton.

Colton- Shooting range today?

Me- Probably not. Gotta finish up an article.

Colton- Dude, I got some inside gossip.

Me- You sound like a chick.

Colton- You won't say that when I'm holding a big ass gun later. Meet me after you drop the girls off.

Me- See you in an hour.

Pulling up to the shooting range, I see Colton's truck already in the parking lot. Damn that fucker is up and going early this morning. I can't imagine what gossip Colton would have I would even be the most remotely interested in. But hell, a morning at the range beats a morning behind the computer.

"Hey fucker, you finally made it," Colton greets me as I walk through the door.

"Whatever asswipe," I tease. "Some of us have responsibilities."

"It's fucking cold this morning. Let's hit up the indoor range."

After firing off some rounds, we stop to reload. "So what's this chick gossip you got?"

"So, I've been talking to Leilani—"

"You drug me to the range to tell me about the girl you're dating," I interrupt.

"Just shut up and listen. Leilani is coming home next week, and her parents are coming with her, but Daniella doesn't know it. They plan on surprising her."

"Dude, what the hell does this have to do with me?"

"They miss their grandson, so they're coming to take him on vacation for the week."

"So?"

"You're lucky you're cute, 'cause you are an idiot, brother. Eva's taking your girls away, right? The Kahele's are taking Aaron."

Oh fuck! Lightbulb.

SINCE THE MOMENT I told Ms. Johnston I would help with the Family Barbeque, she has been on me like a fly on shit. At last count she has called me fifteen times over the last three days. Today she left me a voicemail asking how well I know my meat; the woman freaks me out. I'll be happy when London is out of her class in a couple months.

"Girls! Hurry up. I told Ms. Johnston I'd be there early to help set up. She'll send out a search party if I'm late."

My two beautiful daughters come bouncing down the stairs. "Ready!" They shout together. I really did get lucky with my children. They're smart, beautiful, and well behaved. Most of the time. London leaps off the second to bottom step and into my arms.

"Daddy, Ms. Johnston is so happy your helping. She said you were dreamy. Does that mean she dreams about you?"

"I have no idea honey," I sigh. She should not be saying things like that to my daughter.

"Alright, c'mon. We don't want to be late," Harper starts to rush us out the door.

"What's the rush? Are you meeting Tanner again today?" I ask.

"Nope. It's family day. Plus, Tanner is going out with Amanda now. She likes to steal things from others. Now, let's go!" my oldest shouts.

The entire drive to the school, Harper and London are whispering to each other in the back seat. They're getting along; indication number one something is up. Two, they are both a bit too eager to go to a school function.

"What's going on, girls?" I ask.

"Nothing." London giggles. I see Harper elbow her in the side. Something is definitely up. The whispers and giggles continue the rest of the drive.

"Ok, anyways, while I'm helping Ms. Johnston cook the burgers and dogs, you girls are going to hang out with Daniella and Aaron. So, behave and listen to her until I'm done."

"Why? She's not our family," Harper rudely states.

"Harper Leigh. You will not be disrespectful. I'm sorry your mom couldn't be here, but Daniella has been nice enough to offer to hang out with you girls today."

Thirty minutes later, the festivities are underway and the line for food is starting to grow. My daughters are helping me pass out burgers to all the hungry families while waiting for Daniella and Aaron to get here.

"She's here. She's here," London says.

"What the hell?" I mumble. "Is this what you girls have been whispering about?"

"It's a family day, Dad. Who better to be here than Aunt Nic," Harper informs me.

"Hey, Nicolette," I greet her when she walks up to our grill. "Where's the new husband?"

"Nice to see you too, Connor. He's working. I came down for the weekend to surprise my family."

"I'm sure your parents will be happy to see you," I coldly reply.

"I was talking about you guys."

"Auntie!" London shouts, jumping into her arms.

"Munchkin!" Nicolette spins my daughter through the air. No matter what Nicolette and I are going through at the moment, the connection she has with my daughters is undeniable.

"London, why don't you take Nicolette to meet your teacher while your sister and I finish up serving these dogs.

"Yeah," London agrees. "C'mon, Auntie."

Waiting until they are out of earshot, I do my best not to lay into Harper. I have not heard from Nicolette since the wedding and I was not ready to have her just show up today.

"What the hell is going on here, Harper?"

"I called Nic a couple days ago to ask for some boy advice. She asked how you were. I told her you were good and that you met someone."

"Harper, that is not your business to share," I say, trying extremely hard to keep my cool. "So why is she here and why didn't you tell me?"

"London invited her, and Nic asked us to keep it a surprise."

"Things like this shouldn't be kept from me, sweet pea."

"I'm sorry, Daddy. I thought it would be a cool surprise," she says, deflated.

"Oh, baby, it is. Thank you for trying to do something nice."

"Are you and Aunt Nic ok?"

"We're fine. Let's finish up here and enjoy the day."

"Hey!" Daniella greets us. "Sorry we're late."

"Mana peed on Mommy's new carpet.

"Who's Mana?" I ask.

"He's my new dog! Mommy got me a box dog," Aaron proclaims.

"He's a boxer," Daniella says.

"So, you took my advice and got a dog?"

"I mean, a boy needs a dog right." Her smile can bring any man to his knees.

"Where's London?" Aaron asks.

"Here I am," her bubbly voice interjects.

"Connor, do you want me to grab us some food and find a place to sit?" Nicolette coyly asks.

"Ms. Daniella, this is my Auntie Nic. She came to surprise Daddy today," London says.

"Good to see you again," Daniella says.

"London invited her to surprise me. I had no idea she was coming," I explain.

"The more the merrier." Daniella's happy attitude is a quality I find massively attractive.

"I forgot the chairs in the car. Want to help me grab them?" I ask her.

"Of course. Harper, will you help Aaron get his hot dog?"

"Sure. C'mon kids."

The daggers being shot out of Nicolette's eyes as we walk to the car have me slightly baffled. This is the first time I've seen my best friend since her wedding and our relationship is completely different.

As soon as we are out of sight of the kids, I grab Daniella around the waist and bring her lips to mine. "I have been waiting to kiss you all day."

"You have?" she asks.

"Definitely. I've been thinking about it ever since the morning at the Cottage Lake house." The blushing on her cheeks causes my dick to stir in my jeans. "Damn, woman. You may be the death of me."

"C'mon handsome, let's get back to the get kids."

"And Nicolette," I add, obviously irritated.

"Oh yeah, her too." She laughs.

Walking up the table, I hear London and Nicolette in a rolling belly laugh. "What's so funny, ladies?"

"Remember that time we went camping at the lake and you slipped in the water trying to catch a fish and had to walk around like a wet noodle all weekend?" my youngest asked.

"Yeah, not my finest moment." I laugh.

"Or the time we were in San Francisco and the guy holding the tree branches jumped out and scared you? You screamed like a girl. That was so funny," Harper chimes in.

"My favorite is when we went skydiving for graduation," Nicolette adds.

"I still want to see that video," says Harper.

"You're not old enough to learn the curse words your daddy said that day."

"What is this? Laugh at Dad hour?"

"Well, not at first. Nicolette asked us to share our favorite memories with you," London says.

"We have so many memories together," Nicolette says.

"Yeah, we do. Thirty-one years of them." My best friend and I have been distant since she met and married Brad. I truly do miss her.

"Hopefully, many more," she adds.

"Of course, there will be, Auntie Nic. You're family!" London squeals. "What's your favorite memory with my daddy?" she asks Daniella.

"Hmmm. I haven't known him too long, but I think I would have to say it was the first time I heard him sing karaoke," Daniella says.

"Are you sure it wasn't when we saw the lovebirds at the zoo?" Harper asks.

"We didn't see any lovebirds," London adds.

"Daddy did."

"Enough, Harper." By Daniella's fidgeting, I sense this conversation is making her uncomfortable.

"Little man, girls, want to go get some ice cream?" she asks.

"Sure!" The three kids shout.

"Want me to go with you?" I ask.

"Nope. You stay and visit with your family. Nicolette, nice to see you again."

I watch her ass sway as she walks away, and it takes everything in my power not to chase after her. Instead, I'm left here to confront Nicolette on why she's here.

"What's going on Nic? I haven't heard from you in over a month, then you just show up here and put me on the spot in front of my kids and the woman I just started dating. And obviously, you're not pregnant."

"No, false alarm with all the wedding stress. I'm sorry I haven't called you Connor. I should have. I needed you. I need my best friend."

"We will always be best friends Nicolette."

Teri Kay

CHAPTER TEN

Daniella

"Parallel Lines"

"HEY SISTA," LEILANI'S BOUNCY voice wakes me up. "How'z it?"

"How'z it? It's seven in the damn morning. How do you think I am?" I grumble.

"I'm sorry Dani. I'm just ready to come home. Are you still able to pick us up this afternoon?"

"Us?"

"Me. Able to pick me up."

"You said us."

"No, I didn't. You need coffee. Go wake up and I'll see you later."

"Why can't your lover boy Colton pick you up? It's been a long ass week and I hate driving to the airport."

"Just be at the airport by four. Oh, and bring Aaron and a bigger car. I'm bringing home a lot of baggage."

"What? Why? How am I supposed—"

"Aloha Dani."

Ugh…All I wanted to do was sleep in this morning after my grueling week at work. Brock Hardy said he'd gotten an uncomfortable vibe from the Cottage Lake home but wants to hire me to find him the perfect home. Every day, I scoured the new listings for Brock. The problem is every house I find for him, he finds something he doesn't like about it; not enough light, rooms are too small, yard needs too much work, but my favorite was when he told me there was no cabinet above the toilet for him to rest on when he pees in the morning.

The charm of the young, handsome baseball player everyone falls in love with is hard to resist, but there is something about his cockiness the drives me up a fucking wall. But the young hotshot is shopping for half-million-dollar homes, so I'll put up with whatever attitude he wants to bring to the table.

I'm beyond thrilled Leilani is coming home tonight. Both Aaron and I miss having her here in Seattle with us. All little man can talk about is not having to spend his vacation with the babysitter. As much as he likes Ms. Pam, he complains the older woman smells of stinky cheese and watches weird dog whispering shows.

"Momma!" Aaron shouts, running into my room.

"Good morning, little man. What has you all pumped up?"

"Auntie is coming home today and she said she has a big surprise for me," he squeals. "And I'm on vacation. Where are we going?"

"What do you mean?" I ask, worried about the questions coming next.

"Doesn't vacation mean you get to go somewhere? London says she's going to Florida with her moms, Kevin's going to his dad's in Camiforma, and Ms. Johnston says she's going to Margaritaville."

"Oh, baby, I'm sorry. Work is crazy right now and mommy forgot to plan a vacation for us. We will plan something big for this summer baby."

"Oh. Ok, Mommy. I understand," he says, deflated and disappointed. "I'm gonna go watch TV."

Fuck! How did I completely forget to plan something for Aaron's first spring break? I really am a horrible mother. I'll have to tell Addyson, and Brock, I'm going to take some time off to have a staycation with my son. We'll do the Ferris wheel, the museums and maybe a baseball game.

Addyson asked if she could come over for lunch today. She said she had something she wanted to talk to me about she didn't want to do at the office. Which I thought was silly since it's just her, Josh, and I who share the space. Oh, I wonder if it's something she doesn't want to tell her fiancé about.

As I'm finishing up the salad for lunch, I get a call from Connor. Honestly, I've been missing his voice so I'm glad he called rather than text.

"Hello, handsome," I answer, trying to sound all sexy.

"Hi Ms. Daniella," the happy little voice of London responds to me. "I don't know who handsome is, but this is London. Can I talk to Aaron please?"

"Of course, sweetheart. Aaron, London's on the phone for you."

After a few one word yeah and no's, Aaron asks if we can go to the park with London and her dad. Disappointed, I have to tell my son no again.

"I'm sorry Son, I can't. Aunt Addy is coming over today to talk to mommy about something important."

I listen as Aaron sadly tells his friend we can't go. "Mr. Connor said he'll come pick me up if that's ok Mom? Please. Please. Please."

"Sure, it's fine."

"London, I can go! I'm gonna go get my baseball pants on. See you in a few minutes."

"Mo-oooo-m!" my son shouts.

"What? I'm right here."

"Where are my pants?" He's jumping up and down, more excited than I've seen him in a while.

"In your bottom drawer. You need my help?"

"No, Mom. I can dress myself."

"What's happening to my baby?" I tease.

"Growing up, Momma. Maybe we need another baby." His statement causes me to spit coffee all over the counter. "Eww. Gross Momma."

"Sorry buddy, probably not happening anytime soon."

"Ok. I like just us. And my aunties."

As if on cue, the doorbell chimes. "Speaking of aunties, there's your Auntie Addyson now."

"I'm gonna go change. I don't want to hear your girl talk," he teases me.

"How did you know we sit around talking about how cute boys are?" I say opening the front door.

"I better be the only cute boy you're talking about, missy," Connor says, surprising me.

"Connor. Hey. I was expecting Addy for our lunch date."

He kisses me on the cheek before continuing. "You look beautiful."

"Really? I have no makeup on, my hair's a mess, and I have on yoga pants."

"I know. Turn around," he growls. "I need to see how your ass looks in those pants." I do a twirl to appease him. "Damn, perfection, sweetheart."

"I bet you say that to all the girls." I laugh.

"Only to the ones I like."

"Hey, Connor," Addyson interrupts. "I didn't realize you'd be joining us for girls' lunch today."

"Hey Addy. As honored as I am to be thought of as one of the girls, I just came to get Aaron to take to the park with London before she leaves on Sunday. What time should I have him back by?"

"Three, please. We have to leave by three thirty to pick up Leilani and her massive amounts of luggage. Damn, that reminds me, she told me to bring a bigger car. Where in the world am I supposed to get a bigger car?"

"Take the Denali," he quickly suggests.

"Really? I wouldn't want to inconvenience you."

"When I bring Aaron back, we can switch cars. Plus, then I get to see you again when you return it to me tonight," he says with a wink.

"You really are an angel, aren't you?"

"I can be."

Just as Connor is leaning in to kiss me, we hear Aaron's little feet running down the hallway. "Ready!" he shouts.

"Awesome, little man. London's in the car. Go get buckled in. I'll be right there."

"Bye Mom," Aaron says running down the walkway, without even a look back.

"I'll see you in a couple hours, beautiful," he says, kisses me softly on the cheek and walks to his car.

I close the door behind him and fall to the floor like one of those lovesick teenagers you see in movies. I might possibly even have cartoon hearts swirling above my head.

"Oh, Mr. Rude has really won you over hasn't he?" Addy states.

"He has. I really like him, Addy. Like, like him, like him."

"I know. I saw."

"What? The kiss on the cheek he just gave me?"

"Did something happen at the Cottage Lake house?" she asks.

"Ummm, Connor did show up there. Why?"

"Dani, the home owners have security cameras installed throughout the house. They called and asked why the realtor showing their house was getting fingered in their daughter's bedroom."

"Oh, fuck."

"Yeah, oh fuck is right. This could be bad."

"Addyson, I'm so sorry. You know it's not me to do something like this."

"I know. Mr. Rude seems to be a good influence on you," she jokes.

"Wait? You're not mad?"

"Not at all. Josh and I have done it plenty of times, we just haven't been caught. The homeowners are pissed and say we have the rest of the month to sell the house at asking price or they release the video on the local news and our agency could very well lose its license."

"Consider it done. Damn. There goes the question I was going to ask you."

"Which was?"

"If I could have a couple days off to spend with Aaron on spring break."

"Sure, no problem." She giggles under her breathe.

"What was the giggle for? And if I just royally fucked up with the agency, why aren't you arguing about my time off?"

"No reason. Plus, Josh already thinks he has a buyer for the house, so don't stress out yet. C'mon, since Aaron's gone, let's go grab sushi."

"MOMMY, MR. CONNOR'S CAR is so big compared to yours. Is he rich? Are we poor? Is that why our car is so little?"

"No, Aaron, we are not poor. Mommy just doesn't like driving bigger cars," I explain.

"Then why did we have to bring Mr. Connor's big car? Auntie fits in your car."

"She's bringing home a lot of shit," I say with an attitude, letting Aaron know I am done playing his game of twenty questions.

"Oh! You said a bad word. Dollar in the jar."

"Put on the headphones and watch a movie."

"Yes! I forgot Mr. Connor's rich car has cool stuff like TV's. Rich people stuff," he says.

"Just watch the damn movie."

"Another dollar, Mommy."

"Enough, Aaron." He puts on his headphones and turns on whatever movie London has left in there. He has a happy smile on his chubby little face, obviously very proud of himself for catching me with two inappropriate words today.

With my son finally engaged in a movie, I have a few minutes of quiet time, before Leilani starts filling me in on all the gossip from back home. I am quite looking forward to having my little sister back with me. Having her here is like having a piece of Makoa here with me too.

I need to remember to text Brock when I get home later and see if he could get Aaron and I tickets for an upcoming Brawlers game. I also need to figure out how I'm going to sell the Cottage Lake house at full price. I cannot risk having the video exposed. I wonder if I should share this information with Connor?

So far, Connor's huge SUV has not been difficult to drive, but I have yet to maneuver in and out of the airport. While my sister-in-law was in the air, I sent her a message and told her to be on the lookout for Connor's large vehicle, like she requested.

"Aaron. Help momma out." I hand him my phone. "Push the yellow and white box on the bottom."

"Who am I texting?" he asks.

"How do you know you're texting?"

"Auntie Leilani showed me one day."

"Really? Send her a text and tell her we are here. Do you need me to spell it for you?"

"Momma, those are yellow and green words. Ms. Johnston said we better know how to spell those by first grade."

"You are getting too smart for your own good buddy."

"Ms. Johnston says the same thing, Momma."

Pulling up to Hawaiian Air, I see Leilani's bright pink luggage. She spots me at the same time, jumping up and waving her arms.

"There's Auntie!" Aaron screams from the backseat, bouncing up and down in his booster. "Nana! Papa!" He continues to shout.

"What the fuck?" I say much louder than I intended.

Completely distracted by the fact my in-laws are standing on the curb with Leilani, I hit the car in front of me. "Damn it!" I shout.

"Wow, Momma. Two more dollars. I'm gonna be the rich one soon."

"Enough, Aaron."

I pull over to the loading zone and park the vehicle. "Goodness, Daniella. Are you ok? Is my grandson ok?"

"We're ok." My mother-in-law rushes to give me a hug. "You guys load up the car while I exchange insurance information with this guy."

The first time I borrow Connor's car, I get into a fender bender. I wonder if he's the type to get upset over something like this, because honestly, I don't know him all that well.

Twenty minutes later, we are back on the freeway fighting traffic and then miserable rain to get home.

"What are you guys doing here?" I ask.

"Vacation. Why else?" Lani answers.

"Oh wonderful."

"Thanks for telling me sis," I grumble to Leilani.

"We made her promise to keep it a secret."

"Which I'm not sure why since you guys are only staying here two days," Leilani adds.

"Only two days? Where are you going after that?" I inquire.

"My sister's getting older, so we thought we'd go visit her in Texas while we are all still young enough to enjoy it."

"Whose car is this?" Lani, my father-in-law asks.

"This is Mr. Connor's car. He takes me to the park and plays baseball with me," Aaron pipes up.

"You are going to have to tell me all about this Mr. Connor, now won't you Aaron," Helen says.

"I like Mr. Connor. I think Momma does too."

"Alright everyone. How about the quiet game for a while because Momma has a headache?"

The remaining twenty-minute drive is silent.

As we are unloading the luggage, Helen pulls me aside. "Are you ok?"

"Yea, Helen. I'm just tired. Some things are going on at work and Aaron's sad because all of his friends are going on vacation and he's not."

"About that," she says trailing off and not finishing her sentence.

"Yes?"

"Lani and I would like to take him to Texas with us to meet my family."

"Are you sure? He's six and a handful nowadays."

"He's the spitting image of Mak. I think I'll be fine."

Her words bring tears to my eyes. "I miss him so much." I start to sob in her arms. "He…you were my *ohana*."

"Were? Have we gone somewhere? Dani, you will always be our daughter and will always be our *ohana*."

"Thank you."

"No, thank you, baby girl. You brought my son such joy when you were together. The love between you two was real. You gave us our handsome grandson. Makoa would never want your happiness and beauty to turn cold. He would want you to share your light with all who are willing to accept it. And from what I hear, this Mr. Connor might be the one to do that."

"What did you hear?" I laugh, wiping away my tears.

"Go return his car. We'll catch up after dinner."

Jumping back in the car, I head over to Connor's to return his smashed truck. The closer I get to his house, the more my palms begin to sweat.

"A deer jumped in front of the car. An old lady backed into me. Oh, I got it! There was an alien invasion and they came down to smash the headlights of all the Denali's at Sea-Tac Airport. Ironically, yours was the only one," I mumbled to myself as I drove down his street.

I sit in the driveway for a minute, thinking Canada's not too far off for an escape. Maybe I can just drop the car off, run home and he won't even notice. Crap. What about my car?

A knock on the window sends me flying so high I hit my head on the roof. "Oh my god, Daniella. Are you ok?"

"Ow. Yeah, I'm fine," I say rubbing my head. "Damn, that's the second bump my head's taken tonight."

"Second?"

"Yeah, about that. Ummm. I was in a minor fender bender tonight."

"Holy shit. Really?"

"I'm sorry, Connor. I'll pay for everything."

"Get out of the car, right now," he demands. I feel the tears start to run down my face. I knew he going to be pissed.

I'm thinking I can grab my purse and beeline straight to my Cooper and end this relationship like a rip of a Band-Aid. I jump down and attempt to make my way to my car but am abruptly stopped and spun around to meet the gaze of Connor's intense blue eyes.

"Baby, are you ok? Are you hurt?"

"I'm fine. Your front end is messed up. I'm so, so sorry."

"I don't care. Oh my god, Aaron. Little man's ok, right?"

"Shaken up but fine. He forgot about it the second he saw his grandparents. That's what caused me to freak out and hit the guy in front me. I'm so sorry, Connor."

"Sweetheart, stop. If no one was hurt, it's a car. I couldn't give a shit as long as the precious cargo is safe." He leans down and kisses me softly on the lips. Wrapping his arms around my waist, the kiss deepens and our tongues begin to gently swirl together. Damn, this man makes my heart skip a beat.

"So, how long are Makoa's parents here for?"

"Wait? How do you know it's Mak's parent's and not mine?"

"Ummm. Shit." He smiles and starts kissing me again.

"Did you know?"

"Maybe," he draws out with a mischievous laugh.

"Is this why Addyson was so quick to give me the rest of the week off?"

"Possibly."

"Did Leilani have something to do with all of this?" I inquire.

"Daniella, stop asking questions and just enjoy the fact you're going to get a vacation for a couple of days."

"I wish. It's too late to plan anything. Plus, what would I do? Where would I go? And vacation alone? Who wants to do that?"

"Who said anything about being alone? Go with me to Snoqualmie for a couple days?" he asks.

"Really?"

"Really."

"I'd love to."

Teri Kay

Connor

CHAPTER ELEVEN

"**L**ONDON'S TWISTED HER ANKLE last week in gymnastics, so if it's hurting her then give her the Tylenol I packed in her bathroom bag and even though she won't admit it, she still likes her night-light on to fall asleep. Harper is scheduled to start her period this weekend, so she might be a little cranky."

"Connor, they're still my children. I think they will be fine in my care for a week," Eva snidely retorts.

"You've barely talked to them, no less seen them in the past six months. They've changed. They are growing up."

"I'm sorry. I know. Things have been difficult."

165

"I'm sure living on a tropical island with your lesbian lover is horrible."

"Cut me some slack, Connor. You know it's not like that. My job is hard. Where I was in Thailand was not a tropical island, and Heather left me. Well, I left her after coming home to find her riding some young private's dick."

I feel like an asshole the moment a chuckle escapes my throat. "I'm sorry, Eva."

"It's ok. I guess I deserve it for walking out on true love. Connor, I—" *The Difference* by Tyler Rich interrupts her from my pocket at the perfect moment. "Song ringtones?" My ex-wife questions.

"Hey, sweetheart. You ready?" I ask answering my phone. "Excellent. Was little man excited about Texas? Cool. Eva's here now picking up the girls, so I'll be over to get you shortly."

"Who was that?" Eva questions.

"A friend."

"You call all your friends sweetheart?"

"Once you started sleeping with your secretary, you lost the right to ask what I call my friends, *sweetheart*," I spit back.

"I haven't told the girls yet, but I'll be moving back to Seattle next month."

"Awesome. For how long this time?" I ask.

"For good. I'm leaving the military. It's just not making me happy anymore. Connor?"

"What is it Eva?"

"Could there ever be a chance for us again?"

"Mommy! Mommy!" London comes barreling down the front walkway. "I've missed you so much."

"Me too, pumpkin. Me too."

"Hey Mom," Harper says with much less enthusiasm. "Where's Heather?"

"She stayed back in Thailand. I'll explain later."

"So, it's just you taking care of us?" she asked. Again, a damn chuckle escapes my throat. This time causing me to choke up my Mountain Dew.

"Geez, why does everyone act like I can't take care of my kids?" Eva asks.

"Well," Harper, London, and I say in unison.

"Whatever." Eva laughs. "And no, Aunt Marie and the kids are coming with us, too."

"Yes!" the girls shout.

"Say goodbye to your dad and go put your stuff in the car girls. I need to talk to him for just a minute, and then we'll go."

"Bye, daddy. See you in a week," they both say before giving me hugs and piling off to the car.

"Connor, about what I said before—"

"Stop, before you go any further. I love you, Eva. I always will. You're the mother of my children. But as far as us ever being together again. I don't think so."

"Is this because of your new sweetheart?" she rudely asks.

"No, this is because you divorced me. Have a nice vacation Eva. I'll see you and the girls in a week."

"We could be the perfect family again. Think about it." She leans up and kisses me on the cheek.

"We were never the perfect family," I grumble under my breath.

I lock up the house, drop Bubba off at my parents for a few days, and begin to make my way to Daniella's house. I'm still reeling over my conversation with Eva today. Could she honestly think I'd take her back? I loved Eva for half of my life, but the day she served me with divorce papers was the day I was no longer in love with her.

Why today? She hasn't said anything when we've talked recently on the phone. Was it jealousy hearing I gave someone a custom ringtone? Or the fact I called Daniella sweetheart on the phone? The bigger question is why am I letting it bother me so much?

Pulling up in front of Daniella's house, I can see her watching for me from her front window. Before I even get the car in park and turn off the engine, my girl is already bouncing her way down the walkway toward me. Her smile can make me forget my own name no less any bullshit ideas Eva has in her head.

"Hey," she says.

"Hi. You look mind-blowing." Unable to control myself, I wrap my arms around her waist and take two handfuls of her incredible ass. Daniella has on a pair of skinny jeans showing off every one of her delicious curves, a low-cut top giving me a tempting view of her girls, and her golden blonde hair is perfectly framing her glowing face.

"You're not too bad there yourself, handsome," she teases, reaching around giving my ass a quick grab.

"Come on, let's blow this popsicle stand!" I grab her bag, tossing it in the back with mine. As the back hatch is closing, I see Daniella opening her door to get in the car.

"Stop!" I yell.

"What? What's wrong?" Daniella jumps three feet back from the car and almost falls over the planter box.

"Oh, my goodness, Daniella. Are you alright?"

"Yeah. What the hell Connor?"

"I'm sorry sweetheart, but as long as you're with me, you will never open a door. I'm your gentleman."

"You're kidding, right?"

"Do I look like I'm kidding?" I try to give her my stern face, but I've been told by my daughters it makes me look like I have to take a poop. By the expression on Daniella's face I'm sure she's thinking the same thing.

"Do you need to use the bathroom before we go? Aaron makes the same face when—"

"Get your smart ass up in the car, woman and let's get going."

"We'd already be on the road if you would have just let me open my own door," she quips back.

"Not gonna happen sweetheart."

Within the first thirty minutes of the drive I've learned Daniella is a constant radio flipper with a very random taste in music. We've gone from listening to country, to metal, throwing in a show tune, and ending up on the eighties station. It must be Coke and never Pepsi. She's allergic to strawberries and absolutely cannot stand kale. Her favorite color is purple, and she loves hibiscuses or anything that smells like the flower.

"Do you know how to ski?" I ask.

"No. Is that a problem?"

"Not at all, sweetheart. It just means we'll have to spend some time on the bunny slopes so I can teach you."

"Thanks," she says, almost embarrassed.

"So, no snow vacations as a kid?"

"No vacations as a kid. I was raised by grandmother and we didn't have much money."

"I'd love to hear about it," I tell her.

169

"About what? My childhood?" Daniella questions.

"Yeah, Daniella. I want to know about you and what has made you such a beautiful person."

"You got some rose-colored glasses on there, buddy."

"Doubt it. Share with me who you are, sweetheart."

"At sixteen, my mom got knocked-up by the older guy who lived upstairs from her."

"How much older?"

"He was twenty-one. My mom said she used him to buy her and her friends alcohol. She didn't have anything else, so she'd repay him with sex. Hence, me. My sperm donor had no desire to be a father. He tried for a couple years. One night, my mom went to his apartment to drop me off before she went to work and he was gone. His place was empty."

"Holy shit," I mumble. I feel bad in a way since my childhood was almost textbook perfect. "How did you end up with your grandmother?"

"My mom tried for a few more years. By the time she was twenty-one she was a full-blown alcoholic and decided motherhood was too hard. She hopped in a seventies VW bus and that was the last I saw of her for over ten years."

"Daniella, I'm so sorry."

"Don't be. My grandmother and I had the best life together. It was just me and her. We were broke, but she made every day an adventure."

"Will I get to meet her one day?"

"She died about ten years ago. An hour after her funeral, I got on a plane, never looking back on Boise or my mother."

"Where did you go then?"

"Seattle. I found a room for rent, met some great friends, and decided to become a real estate agent."

"So how did you end up in Hawaii?" She explains the story of her cheating douchebag ex-boyfriend and how the impulsive move to Hawaii became the best decision of her life.

"Going out to karaoke with Addyson a couple months ago is turning out to be another one of those one-eighty changes in my life." Daniella reaches over, intertwines her fingers with mine giving me a smile letting me know we're on the same page.

Pulling up to the hotel, I watch Daniella's eyes grow wider. This hotel has been on Washington's must stay list for the past eight years in a row.

"This place looks like a castle," she says in awe.

"Welcome to Kodiak Peak," the valet greets us, opening Daniella's door. "Check-in is through those doors and your bags will be delivered to your room shortly."

"C'mon, let's go get checked in so we get to our dinner reservation on time."

"Connor, you really didn't have to do all this."

"Of course, I did. Do you know how long it's been since I've met a girl I wanted to impress?"

"You're doing a damn excellent job, Mr. Evans," she softly says.

"Wait until you see what I have in store for this weekend," I say in a low gruff tone causing goosebumps to pop up on her arms.

"Next," the concierge yells.

"Hi, reservation for Evans." I hand her my ID and she begins punching away on her keyboard.

"You have two rooms for three nights," she confirms.

"Correct. They are adjoining?"

"Yes sir, they are. Suite 804 and room 805. Here are your keys and the bellhop will bring up your bag within the next twenty minutes."

I waited until we were in the privacy of the elevator to ask her why the tears were forming in her eyes.

"Because you thought enough about me to get us separate rooms," she says.

I want this to be a fun, relaxing weekend; no tears. Time to lighten the mood. "Oh, honey, don't think I got an extra room for you. I mean this is technically our first real date. I'm not sure I'm ready for you to see the onesie yet."

"You don't have a onesie." She giggles.

"Oh, just you wait and see."

"Daniella, this weekend is about having fun and getting to know each other. There will be no pressure, sweetheart. I promise you."

"I'm looking forward to spending time with you," she says almost in a purr.

"Here's your key."

"Connor, I am not taking the suite. You paid for all this. You should have it."

"Wait till you see the bathroom."

"Sold!" She laughs.

"Your laugh is so sexy. You know that?"

"Really? I've never liked it. I snort when I'm tickled."

"That's a secret you should have kept to yourself, sweetheart," I warn her.

"C'mon, let's check out our rooms."

We enter Daniella's two-room suite first. The front room is divided into a simple sitting area with a couch and a television much too large for the small room and a basic kitchen. But it's the bedrooms in the suites which makes this hotel such a high commodity. They have the largest beds, covered in only the highest quality linens, built for the comfort of a king. The adjoining bathroom wall has a magnificent gas fireplace, which can be enjoyed from both the bed and the deep jacuzzi tub.

"Connor this is insane. I don't think I have ever seen anything so beautiful before."

"I have." I spin her around and take control of her mouth. My tongue is on a mission to make hers submit to mine. My hands take a tight grip around the back of her neck, forcing our connection to deepen.

I feel Daniella's hands slide into my T-shirt, her nails ever so gently run a trail along my sides. I'm instantly caught between being completely turned on and nervous as fuck. Even though I'm confident as a bigger guy, the first time getting naked with a woman can be intimidating. Yet, I am dying to get naked with this exquisite creature standing before me.

Reluctantly, we pull apart, both needing to come up for air. Her big blue eyes are staring back at me with a look I've only seen from Daniella once before. She starts nibbling on her bottom lip causing my dick to stir in my jeans.

"What, sweetheart?" I ask.

"Never mind," she says, "Let's go check out your room." She tries to spin out of my arms, but there is no way in hell I'm letting that happen.

"What is going through your curious mind?"

"How important are those dinner reservations you had tonight?"

"Why? Is there something else you'd like to do?" Daniella's

face turns five different shades of red with my question. "Damn, you're cute when you blush." Almost instinctively, I lean down and kiss both her cheeks. "Now tell me what you're thinking."

"The last few weeks have been draining and I'm exhausted. I would love to just relax, sit in a hot tub, and enjoy the fire with a nice bottle of wine."

"They are completely negotiable, baby. How about I order us some room service instead?"

"Sounds perfect," she purrs.

"So, after we eat and get our luggage, I'll let you relax and enjoy your evening."

"Wait? What? You're leaving me?"

"You never said you wanted me to join you in a relaxing, fireside bath, so I just assumed..." I teasingly trail off.

Daniella pushes her body against mine, throwing her arms around my neck. "Wanting you with me should have been a given," she whispers against my lips.

"Good to know." I laugh.

"Connor, I want to be here with you. In fact, I need to be here with you. I like you. I like you a whole hell of a lot. I can't promise you I'm ready for a relationship or I'm not going to freak out from time to time while trying to figure out what I'm doing. But for now, I need to be with you. I need you to touch me, not like I'm some broken, widowed, single mom you need to be delicate with, but as a woman who is longing for the touch and passion of a man; to feel what she's beginning to forget."

I don't think I've ever wanted to be with a woman more than I do with Daniella at this moment. Screw being nervous or self-conscious. Tonight, will be all about making my woman feel like the sexual creature she is.

Scooping Daniella up in my arms, I gently toss her onto the plush comforter covering the bed. I cage myself on top of her, forcing intense eye contact between us.

"I plan on taking care of your every need in the next few days," I say, leaning down to place gentle kisses along her jawline.

A loud knock at the door interrupts our perfect moment. "Bellhop." We hear through the closed door.

"I'll be right back. Don't move," I instruct her.

"Sure." She smiles, giving me the impression she has something else in mind.

It takes close to five minutes for me to get the luggage squared away with the young kid who decides to become Chatty Cathy tonight. I'm disappointed to walk back into Daniella's room and find her bed empty.

To my left, I hear her clear her throat to capture my attention. There stands my blonde beauty in nothing but a white robe, dipping her toes into the hot bubble bath she's prepared.

"Care to join me?" Daniella asks dropping the robe, leaving me looking at her insanely perfect naked body.

"You are gorgeous, baby."

"Thank you." She slowly sinks her body down in the tub finding the naturally grooved seat.

"Oh. My. God," she moans.

"Feel good?" I ask, sounding like an idiot right after the words leave my mouth. Her look of pure relaxation makes the answer obvious.

"Are you going to join me or just stand there like a weird creeper?"

"I don't know, I kinda like watching you, Daniella."

"There you go saying my name again."

175

"Because it's just as sexy as you are."

"Connor, please get in," she requests.

"Before I do, I need you to understand something."

"Yes?"

"I've been thinking about being naked with you since the day at the Cottage Lake house. Once I get in this tub with you, I may not be able to control myself."

"Kind of what I'm hoping for."

CHAPTER TWELVE
Daniella

I NEED CONNOR IN this tub with me. Now.

Mr. Rude has turned out to be nothing like I expected. The night I met him at Slick's, he came off as a pompous ass who I'd rather kick in the balls than ever have a drink with. Then seeing him with his daughters, this giant teddy bear of a man appears. And after our ride on the Ferris wheel and the hot little tryst last week, my desire for Connor Evans has been constantly growing.

I have no idea if I'm ready to jump into another relationship right away, but I damn sure know I'm horny. I mean, I'm a woman who's in the sexual prime of her life and I haven't had sex in almost

177

two fucking years. My friendly little battery-operated buddy hasn't been cutting it for a while now.

I miss the touch of a man; a firm grip on my ass, the tickling of my clit, and especially the popping sound when a man pulls his mouth off my nipples. There are so many things a woman can take care of herself; sucking on your own tits is not one of them.

The sudden look of trepidation on Connor's face is making me question whether inviting him in was the right decision.

"Are you ok? You don't have to get in if you don't want to," I tell him.

"Of course, I want to. Why? Have you changed *your* mind?"

"Not at all. You just look like you may be second guessing my invite."

"Remember how you felt that night in the hot tub?" he asks.

"Yeah. Your confidence encouraged me to take the cover-up off and feel sexy again."

"Alcohol and board shorts can create a bit of confidence to hide behind."

The fact Connor is feeling nervous getting naked in front of me is sexy as all hell. He always comes off as so strong and sure of himself. To see this soft vulnerable side makes me want him even more. Now it's time to show him.

I slowly stand up and let the bubbles drip down my naked body. I can't help but notice Connor's hard dick pressing against his jeans. Wet and still naked, I climb out of the tub and stand in front of this amazingly sexy man.

Grabbing the ends of his shirt, I rise onto the tips of my toes to pull it over his head and off his body. I begin placing soft kisses across his chest.

"I think everything about you is sexy," I whisper. "You were so giving with me last week. It's my turn now."

Dropping to my knees, I am ready to show Connor Evans just how hot I really think he is. It takes just mere seconds to free his already hard cock from his pants. "Damn," I practically growl.

I bring my lips to the pink tip of Connor's dick, placing a few gentle kisses on his head. As I run my tongue up and down his long shaft, I can already feel his excitement growing.

"Fuck, your mouth feels even better than I dreamt it would," he says.

"You've dreamed about me sucking your dick?" I look up at him with those 'I know exactly what I'm doing to you eyes'.

"I've dreamt about it almost every night since I first saw you at Slick's." Connor runs his fingers through my hair, gently encouraging me to take his cock deeper. I allow him to take control as we start moving together in a perfect rhythm.

We both let out a simultaneous moan as I feel his dick begin to throb in my mouth. Feeling he's ready to cum has caused me to become just as excited. I take one hand and start pumping his shaft with the rhythm of my mouth and use the other to start playing with my own clit.

"Daniella, you're gonna make me cum, sweetheart," he moans.

"So, cum." I giggle.

"Already?" he asked, a bit surprised.

"Baby, this is round one. We have three days together." With those words, Connor takes a firm grip of my head and creates the exact pace he needs to fill my mouth with his warm, salty cum.

"That was fucking gorgeous, Daniella," Connor says. "My turn." Pulling me up to my feet, Connor assumes my previous position. With how turned on I am by this man, I know I will have my release in no time. A few laps of his tongue and a quick bite to my clit has me cumming just as quickly as he did.

"Grab those beers and let's enjoy this glorious tub," I say.

The next morning, I wake up to gentle fingers brushing my messy hair from my face. "Good morning, beautiful."

"Oh, there is no way I look beautiful right now," I moan. As I stretch my arms behind my head, I realize my boob has popped out of the sexy cami I wore to bed. Grabbing the sheet, I attempt to cover myself up.

"Don't you dare cover up these beauties." He leans downs and kisses each breast. I moan and arch my back, letting him know he can keep his mouth right where it is.

"You like?"

"So, fucking much." With my comment, he pulls off with the popping sound which drives me fucking crazy. "Ummm…I didn't say you could stop." I laugh.

"As much as I want to devour every inch of this delectable body, we have a ski lesson in a couple hours."

"Really?"

"Yup. So, get your sexy ass up and get ready. We leave for the lodge in an hour."

Luckily, being a single mom, I have learned to be low maintenance, and getting ready takes no time at all. Especially for a day outdoors. I'm ready in half the time Connor gave me.

I expect to find him waiting for me in the sitting area, but it is empty. I peek into his room, but again no Connor. Where the hell did he disappear to? Then I hear shuffling on the balcony.

"Hey!" I surprise him, popping my head out the door.

"Shit," he says, scrambling to hide his cigarette.

"You're a big boy, Connor. You can smoke if you want to."

"I hide my smoking from my kids, so it's habit."

"You don't hide it from me very well," I tease. "I tasted it on your lips the night in the Ferris wheel."

"You did?"

"I did. And it was fucking sexy."

"Really, now?" He pulls my body to his and my insides quiver.

"Or maybe it was just you." I lean in, smashing my lips to his. Connor's moans are the sexiest thing I've heard in months.

"As much as I hate to say this, we have a ski date with Jackie," he says.

"Jackie?" I sarcastically question.

"She was the only instructor available."

"For your sake, you better hope she's ugly." I laugh.

"Damn, it's cute when your possessive." Connor bops my nose and kisses my forehead. "C'mon, let's go bruise our asses."

It takes about an hour to get fitted with our rental equipment and we're told to wait in the lobby for our instructor. Watching others leave with their instructors, it's hard not to notice all the people who work here are extremely good looking. Suddenly, this Jackie chick has me worried and I haven't even met her yet.

We're the only couple left in the room, when a hunk of a man enters through the instructors' door. I'm guessing over six-foot, shoulder length, wavy blonde hair, and these emerald green eyes to die for. I think this guy walked out of one of the books I just read.

"Connor and Daniella," he calls.

"What happened to Jackie?" Connors asks.

"I am Jacques. It's French. People often confuse it," he explains. "It's ok. Let's go ski."

181

"Awesome." I hear Connor mumble under his breath.

"What's up?" I can't help but smile, knowing exactly what's up.

"Nothing," he grumbles.

"I call bullshit. You were just fine when you thought our instructor was going to be Little Miss Snow Bunny."

"You're right, but did our instructor really need to be Thor, the French Ski God?"

"Maybe he'll keep my booty from getting too bruised."

"His hands better be nowhere near your booty, sweetheart. Protecting your ass is my job."

It's taken me a few hours to finally get the hang of skiing. My legs are exhausted and I think my ass is partially frozen.

"You ready to try one of the bigger slopes?" he asks.

"I don't know. I'm not sure how much more falling my ass can handle."

"You're doing great. C'mon, one more and then we'll call it a day."

"Let's do it."

Once at the top of a run named Easy Come Easy Go, I realize the slope is much steeper than anything I previously skied today. As the nerves creep into my stomach, a seven-year-old kid pushes by me and zooms straight down the hill.

"If the kid can do it, so can I." My pep talk gives me this sudden burst of confidence and I begin my descent down the slope.

Halfway down the hill, my momentum grew and I completely forgot everything Jacques and Connor taught me earlier. My ski's cross, I lose my balance and fall forward, slamming my face in the snow.

182

"Oh my god! Daniella!" Connor screams, coming up behind me. He pops his skis off and pulls me to my feet. "Baby! Oh my god, you're bleeding. Can you stand? Do I need to get first aid?"

"Nah, I think I'm fine. Where am I bleeding?"

"Looks like you split your lip. C'mon, let's get you back to the hotel."

All afternoon Connor has doted on my every need. Tended to my wounds, iced my sore muscles, and even found the softest things on the room service menu to feed me lunch. I am literally fighting back getting all teary eyed. It has been the longest time since someone has taken care of me like this. I have always been the one taking care of everyone else.

Coming back in from his cigarette, Connor catches me wiping a tear from my eye. "I thought I said no crying this weekend," he teases.

"Happy tears. I promise. It's just been a while since someone has taken care of me."

"Hold that thought."

During the five minutes I'm left waiting for whatever Connor is doing back in his room, I start realizing how incredible this man is and how lucky I am to be here with him. Maybe everyone is right, maybe it is time to move on. Maybe Connor Evans is the perfect guy to move on with.

And then I see it. Holy shit. He wasn't joking. Watching this goofy man dance toward me in a giant red onesie, the giggles start and by the time he reaches my doorway, I'm in a full-on belly laugh.

"Told you it was real." He joins in on my laughter.

"Now I've seen it all," I say.

"Nope." He reaches around, unbuttons the clasp, and shows me his bare ass. "Now you've seen it all."

Teri Kay

"Come here, goofball." I reach my hand out to pull him to me.

"Did you just call me a goofball?" he asks.

"Yes, I did. What are you going to do about it?"

"You're asking for it now woman." Connor jumps on the bed, caging himself on top of me.

Our eyes connect, and I can't help but become completely mesmerized by his stare. Yet it's not the color of his vibrant blues that has me dazed this time, but a complete tenderness. Like him and I are the only two people in this world.

When he leans down to kiss me, I wince from the pain of my fat lip. "Damn, baby. I'm sorry. Should we stop? I don't want to hurt you?"

"Don't you dare stop. You'll just have to find places other than my lips to kiss."

Connor pulls my shirt off and throws it on the floor next to us. "Your tits are fucking amazing." Without hesitation, he brings his mouth down to my already erect nipple and gently teases it with his tongue.

"Mmmm, you like to tease, don't you?" I say with a breathy moan.

"Whatever do you mean, my dear?" He laughs in between alternating flicks. "Is this what you want?" He asks, just before launching a full tongue assault on my tits.

"Fuck, yes." I moan arching my back to let Connor know this is exactly what I want. I reach down to take hold of Connor's erection pressing into my leg, to let him know I am so ready to take this to the next level, when I realize he is still fully dressed in his silly onesie. "Lie down," I instruct.

"Oh, commands from the older woman. I like that."

I straddle myself across his body and slowly start undoing each button. I make my way all the way down the leg and pull the onesie off his body. Standing at the end of the bed, I take in the naked man lying on the bed in front of me.

Connor is different from the few men I've had sex with in my lifetime. Jimmy was gorgeous and totally into keeping up his appearance, because by nature, that's what real estate agents do. Makoa was a Hawaiian marine. Need I say more? Connor is a bigger bald man. Not someone I would typically say I'd be attracted to, but I am.

I'm attracted to the blue eyes you can see sparkling from across the room, but the smolder he knows how to give with them is panty melting. You can't help but smile when you're with him and he wouldn't have it any other way. And I am completely infatuated with his bald head. In a way I didn't think possible, this man is everything I'm attracted to.

"Everything ok?" he asks. Shit maybe I was staring at him longer than I thought.

"Yeah, everything is perfect." I walk over to the nightstand drawer and grab one of the condoms I hid in there when we first got here.

"Already? No foreplay?" he asks.

"This whole weekend has been foreplay, baby. I am so ready to make love to you," I reply. Fuck! I said the "L" word. In my head I kept reminding myself to say fuck instead of make love. Apparently, I psyched even myself out.

"Are you wet?" he asks, in a deep sultry voice I haven't heard before.

"Maybe you should check as I put this condom on your cock." Before I can even rip the package open, Connor's fingers are pulling my panties to the side and two fingers easily glide in my slick entrance.

"Damn, baby. You are wet," he says and he continues to slide his fingers in and out of my begging pussy.

As I roll the condom on, a flash of nerves race through my body. Fuck. As much as I want this, can I do it? But when Connor's free hand reaches up and rolls my nipple between his fingers, I know I'm ready to climb on and fuck the shit out of this man.

"You ready?" he asks. I smile and nod. "Come here, my fine-ass Daniella." I position myself, so Connor's dick is just tickling the entrance of pussy. "Now look who's teasing. You better slide your tight pussy down my cock right now, before I flip you over giving your ass the spanking it deserves."

"Are you threatening me?" I giggle.

"It's a promise, baby." Before I get the chance to slide down, Connor thrusts his hips, burying his cock deep inside me.

"Shit!" I scream much louder than I intend, throwing my head back in pure ecstasy. We lace our hands together and begin to find a perfect flow. The way Connor fills me gives me a completeness I realize I've been missing.

"My turn," he growls. "Up on all fours," he says in a commanding tone which practically makes me cum right there. He stands at the edge of the bed and waits. "Bring your beautiful ass here."

Umm, does he want to fuck me in the ass? I am sure as hell not ready for ass play yet. "Connor, I'm not sure—" Mid-sentence, he grabs my hips, pulls me back and slams his dick into my pussy, finding our connection once again.

"Your pussy feels too fucking incredible for me to want anything else, my gorgeous Daniella."

"Connor!" I scream.

"Say my name again, sweetheart."

"Connor! I'm gonna cum."

"Wait. Don't cum until I tell you."

"Baby, I don't think I can. You feel too good."

"Not yet, Daniella," he says almost sternly. He continues to move his cock in and out of my pussy causing every part of my body to quiver. "Tell me what you want, beautiful?"

"I want to cum."

"How bad?"

"So, fucking bad!"

"Cum, Daniella. Cum for me." With a few strong thrusts our bodies tremble and pulse together.

He pulls out and I fall on my stomach, spent and out of energy. I hear Connor in the bathroom cleaning up and I wonder if I should get up and do the same, but I just can't get my body to move. I'm attempting to muster up the energy to get up when Connor surprises me by rubbing the warm washcloth against my sensitive pussy.

"Want to go out to dinner?" he asks.

"I was thinking we could stay in and have dessert over and over again."

Teri Kay

Conner
CHAPTER THIRTEEN

I HAVE LITTLE DESIRE to get back to reality. The past three days with Daniella have been better than I ever could have imagined. If there was a way for me to slow down time, I would; I need more time with her. More just us. The girls aren't coming home until tomorrow, so I'm hoping she'll stay one more night with me.

Halfway home, Daniella gets a call from Addyson. She rejects the call saying she'll talk to her when she gets home because work will not interrupt our time together. But her boss is persistent and calls three more times.

189

"Addy, what's up? I'll be home in an hour," Daniella answers.

Not if I can help it, I think to myself.

"Shit, really? Alright. I know." I can see the distress on her face while listening to her boss. "I'll figure it out. How much longer do we have? Alright. I'll get it sold." She hangs up and throws her phone in her purse.

"Sweetheart, what's wrong?"

"As sexy as our little adventure was last week, it may cost me my license and humiliate and ruin my best friends' business."

"What are you talking about?"

"There were cameras, Connor. If I don't sell the Cottage Lake house in the next three weeks for full price they are going public with the tape."

"Don't you think this is something you should have told me?" I ask, slightly irritated she would keep this from me.

"I was hoping this sale would go through and I wouldn't have to, but as you heard, it didn't, and I have three weeks to sell the house."

"You're in this mess because of me, baby. I will do everything I can to help you sell this house."

"What did I do to deserve you?" she asks.

"I keep asking myself the same question." The smile Daniella puts on my face is undeniable. "When does Aaron come home from Texas?"

"Tomorrow. The girls?"

"Same. Let's spend one more night together. Sleep in my bed with me?"

"I'd love to."

"Do you need to go home for anything?"

"Nope."

"Awesome. I am so ready to spend the night messing up my sheets with you."

"You are insatiable, Mr. Evans." She giggles.

"That's because you're delectable, Ms. Daniella."

"Does this thing go any faster?" she teases.

No sooner do Daniella and I close the front door of my house, our hands are invading every inch on each other's body.

"I need you inside me. Please, Connor, make love to me again?"

"Anything you desire, sweetheart." I swoop her up in my arms and carry her to my room.

"Oh, my goodness! Put me down."

"I'll put you down, alright." I place her down next to my bed. "Get naked."

"Yes, sir."

Daniella sits down on the edge of the bed, begins to slowly unzip and remove her knee-high boots; something about a woman undoing a zipper is sexy as hell to me. Moving like molasses, she lifts one leg in the air and pulls the leggings off her body and throws them on the floor.

"You do like to tease, don't you?" I growl.

"Am I not moving fast enough for you, Mr. Evans?"

I stand in front of her to offer my assistance with the removal of her shirt, but she playfully swats my hands away at each attempt. She laces our fingers together to take control of the situation and I gladly give it to her.

"Tell me what you want, Connor," she says in a husky demanding voice causing my dick to immediately spring into action.

"I want you, Daniella. All of you."

She reaches down, grabs the hem of her shirt, and pulls it off. Daniella throws herself back on the bed, leaving me staring at this magnificent creature in front of me in her matching black panties and bra.

"Take me," she boldly states.

In two seconds flat, I'm standing naked in front of her ready to go. But Daniella's not like any other woman I've ever been with before. I want to take my time and enjoy every second with my woman. I need to worship her body.

I start by kissing her ankles and working my way up her gorgeous thick thighs. Locking my finger on the sides of her panties, I yank the silky material off and add them to the pile forming on the floor. She unhooks her bra, adding it to the pile.

"I could stare at your insane body all night long."

"I'd rather you play with it." She giggles.

"Your wish is my command, beautiful."

Continuing, I devour her body, my tongue gently swirls along the inside of her pussy, just long enough to allow her taste to linger on my tongue.

"Damn, you are fucking delicious." Her nails run along the top of my head encouraging me to continue what I'm doing.

I kiss my way up her tempting body and find my way to her perfect breasts. I push the beautiful mounds together and flick my tongue between each nipple. She grabs the headboard behind us and arches her back pushing her tits further into my mouth.

"Mmmm," she moans. "You make my body feel incredible."

"You think this is incredible, just wait until I'm inside you."

"Please don't make me wait any longer, Connor."

"Anything for you my Daniella."

I reach over and grab the condom off the nightstand and roll it on my aching dick. "I'm so ready for you, baby."

I take Daniella's arms and hold them over her head, I softly nibble along her jawline, causing her body to shake underneath mine. I slide into her soft and begging wetness. We simultaneously let out a noise which sounds like a mix between a moan and a scream.

I start out slow, but quickly increase my pace unable to control myself when I'm with her.

We spend the next hour teasing and pleasing each other in every way we think possible. Exhausted and starving, we finally leave the bed in search of food.

"How does breakfast sound? Eggs, bacon, and potatoes?" I ask.

"Sounds fantastic!"

"Go find something on television. I'm gonna return a video chat from the girls and then I'll start cooking."

"Oh, it's Friday night. Live P.D.," she squeals.

"Perfect."

I set my phone up in the kitchen, so I can start cooking while talking to my daughters. On the second ring, I am surprised when Eva answers and not Harper.

"Hey Connor. The girls are at the pool with Marie," my ex explains.

"Oh, ok. Have them call me when they get back."

"Of course. Connor, you have done such an amazing job with our girls. You are raising them to become fine young women."

"Thanks. I'm trying."

"What about trying with me? Have you given what I said any thought?"

"Actually, I haven't thought about it at all."

"Connor, I made a huge mistake. I have loved you half of my life and I want to continue loving you. For us, for our family. Don't you want to be a family again?"

"My daughters and I will always be a family, Eva. Please tell them I called." I quickly hang up the phone, not wanting to deal with her bullshit any longer.

"So, Eva wants you back? What happened to Heather?" Daniella asks, standing in the kitchen doorway.

"Apparently, she was found riding the dick of some young private and Eva left her."

"Why didn't you tell me about this?"

"I don't know. I didn't think my ex-wife's sex life was something we needed to talk about on our weekend away. Just like you didn't think telling me we got caught on video was important."

"Eva's also decided she's leaving the army and moving back."

"Wait, she's moving back to Seattle?"

I sense her trepidation. I've never heard Daniella's voice shake before. My response is interrupted by Bubba's barking, which alerts us to someone coming up the walkway.

I look through the peephole to see what I'm in for before answering. What the hell? What is she doing here?

"Nicolette? What the hell are you doing here?"

"Wow. What a way to greet your best friend?"

"Best friend? I have only heard from you once since you married Brad. Speaking of Brad is he here with you this time?" I ask.

"Well," she takes a deep breath and sighs. "That's kind of why I'm here. Can I come in?"

"Honestly, Nicolette, I have company at the moment." I don't think I have ever been so cold to my best friend.

"Is it Daniella?" she asks.

"It doesn't matter who it is, Nic. Why are you here when you should be home with your husband?"

"I left him, Connor."

"You did what? Why would you do something like that?"

"Because Connor, I don't love Brad. I'm...I'm in love with you. I think I always have been. I need to know the 'what ifs' about us. Can there be a chance for us?" she begs.

"Like I said Nic, I have company tonight. Maybe you and I should talk about this another night," I suggest.

"We've known each other our whole lives and you've known her, what, like five minutes? And you're going to choose some wedding floozy over your own best friend?"

"Enough. Why are you being like this?" I ask.

"I made a mistake letting you get away once by not seeing what was right in front of me all along. I can't make that same mistake again."

Out of the corner of my eye, I catch Daniella putting on her shoes. "Where are you going?" I run over to her, taking the second shoe from her hand.

"I called Leilani. She's on her way to pick me up," she explains.

"Baby, please don't leave."

"I think it's best I do. Obviously, you two have a history I can't compete with. And I just don't think I'm ready for the kind of relationship you want. And I sure as hell don't need the drama of an ex-wife and a best friend." The tears stream down her face and I hate that it's me breaking her heart.

"Daniella, that's not true." But I didn't even sound convincing to myself. Before she can say anything else, Leilani honks her horn from the driveway.

She grabs her bag, rushes past Nicolette and jumps in the car before I can stop her.

Nicolette stops me in the doorway. "Let her go, Connor. Maybe things are working out the way they're supposed to." The smug smile on her face reminds me of someone who has just stolen candy from a baby.

As Leilani's car backs out of the driveway, I lock eyes with Daniella and I feel like my world has just done another one-eighty.

To be continued...

First and foremost, I want to thank my readers and fans. It's because of you all, I keep doing this. There have been a few times when I thought I was ready to walk away from this, but then I get a message or see a review about how much you enjoyed reading one of my books and it pushes me keep going.

Kevin, I dedicated this book to you because you are my saving grace in a world that can be extremely difficult to navigate. I love you more than words can say.

Joshua, thank you for being you. I knew immediately that I wanted you on a cover. I didn't have any ideas for a story, but I knew I wanted you. You've given me ideas and input along the way and made writing this book a hell of a lot of fun! I am so glad we've become friends.

Tiffany, you will always be my PIC and best friend. You made such a beautiful cover this story. I'm so proud of to say you designed this cover. Thank you for always be there for me. Love you girl!

Reggie Deanching, it has been so wonderful working with you! Thank you for shooting Joshua and giving us a fresh look with models. I'm looking forward to working with you again.

Rox, you continue to amaze me with your superb editing skills. You know exactly how to push me. I cannot be more grateful for you. I'm so glad the world brought us together. I wouldn't want to do this without you.

Renee at Porcelain Paper Designs, thank you for making the inside of book so beautiful. The time you take formatting my stories is so appreciated. You have become one of my best friends and I'm so happy to have you in my life.

Christina, it's your words that people first read and draw them in. Thank you for creating an awesome blurb that's grabbing everyone's attention.

Colleen, my PA extraordinaire! Thank you for pimping, sharing and having my back in this crazy book world. I'm proud to call you my friend. My next goal is write a book that is going to make cry. I think I have just the story!

Jessica Barnes, this is the first time we've worked together, and I'm thrilled to have your artwork in my story. The chapter headers you've drawn are exactly what I was looking for. Thank you so much.

Nichole, no matter what we will always be there for each other. You came into my life for a reason and I love the bond we share! Thank you so much for being you.

Aimey, thank you all for your love and friendship. Your support and help with each book means so much to me. I love you friend.

Heather L., there was a little part in here just for you. We don't take kindly to thieves around these parts! I'm so happy I always have you to talk to! Love you!

My Sisters of Word Porn, the bond we share is unbreakable. Renee, Kristine, Nichole and Thia, you all are the sisters I've never had. I will always thank Denver for bringing us together!

Misty and Robin, your help with my readers group and sharing my stuff every day is beyond appreciated! It's your pimping that is helping my books get to more readers and I love you for that!

My friends and family, thank you all for listening me endlessly talk about my books and this crazy author life I lead. I know I overshare and you all take it like champs.

Made in the USA
Columbia, SC
09 November 2020

24235522R00109